# NEVER A FAIRY TALE

A Teen Atheist's Conversion to Christ

DANIELLE RENEE WALLACE

ISBN: 978 1 7334039 4 8 (paperback)

*To my loving family. Truly, I'm forever blessed to have been raised in a Christian home. I also dedicate this to all I've come to love so dearly in Ohio and my brethren in Christ across the world. My friends, this story is for you.*

# Table of Contents

# Part 1

*I cannot fit in this new scene*
*I am a misplaced puzzle piece*
*Your faith I call a fairy tale*
*Yet your joy is hardly frail.*

# A Misplaced Puzzle Piece

## Chapter 1

A new town, a fresh start.

Or was it?

Parker Everson sighed as he exited his dad's big, black pickup and waved goodbye. After, he walked toward the high school.

Against the azure morning sky, the sun was bright and hot. Forests of green trees surrounded the buildings of the town, and seas of orange daylilies bloomed everywhere.

Since Parker's parents had just divorced, he and his dad had moved from Wyoming to Ohio.

Currently, he was trying to adjust to everything. The change of scenery, a new house, and being without a mom left him feeling overwhelmed. With worry, Parker also wondered if he'd make any friends here or if he'd be forever lonely.

In Wyoming, he'd lived in a two-story house which resembled something of a fancy log cabin. With tall mountains in the background, it had been his idea of a picture-perfect home. The endless woods in Ohio and mostly flat atmosphere, save for the hills and ridges, were a contrast, and though he thought they were pretty, it was still going to take a while to adjust.

Summer vacation had just ended, and Parker was starting his freshman year of high school. He pushed open one of the double-doors of the building and entered. Myriads of students were bustling around, chatting in groups. Parker's stomach somersaulted as a pang of loneliness jolted through him. These other teens had likely known each other since childhood. Already having plenty of buddies, they wouldn't feel a need to add him to their group. Some people don't have time for new friends.

Feeling very out of place, Parker pressed his lips together in a firm line and, using his schedule, found his upcoming class by himself—biology. He wasn't in Wyoming anymore, and he was sure his friends there would likely soon forget about him. Now, he didn't feel like he belonged anywhere. In his hometown, life would go on without him. And here, he would stand on the sidelines, watching other people's lives unfold while he was stuck as a mere onlooker.

*This is all Mom's fault,* Parker thought bitterly. *I'm just a misplaced puzzle piece now—one that can't fit in any picture. I'm not made to complete the design.*

He slumped in one of the backrow seats of the biology class and ran a hand through his light-brown hair. Having seated himself early, Parker was the only student inside. The teacher, Mr. Granger, had greeted him politely, but was now looking over his material, leaving Parker to sit in silence.

In the classroom, the walls were painted a boring white, but there were lots of large, clean windows to look out of, which gave a view of the vivid-blue sky and the woods.

Eventually, students began entering and taking seats. A couple of boys in the row directly in front of Parker whispered together loudly, and he realized, with humiliation, that they were talking about him.

"New boy," one whispered with a snobby laugh. "I heard one of the teachers say he's from Wyoming."

"Probably a country bumpkin," the other boy replied. "I bet he has some weird accent."

"Everyone has an accent of some kind, Jeb," a girl with her arms full of schoolwork said as she entered. She looked disapprovingly at the two teasing boys, then turned to Parker with bright-blue eyes—eyes colored like the sky out the window.

"Hi there!" she chirped with a warm smile, thumping her schoolwork on her desk. Holding out a hand to shake, she introduced herself. "I'm Grace McClintock. What's your name?"

"Parker Everson," Parker mumbled, flimsily shaking her hand and feeling self-conscious. No one had talked directly to him except the teacher until now. Noticing his awkwardness, the two boys who had been making fun of him snickered.

Grace had pretty, brown hair, which she currently wore in a messy bun. A light sprinkling of freckles was scattered across her nose, and Parker noted she had a very cheerful disposition. She hadn't stopped smiling.

"It's nice to meet you, Parker," Grace said, and there was a sincere tone in her voice. "You're from Wyoming, right? I think that's fun—I've always wanted to go there! My family and I went to Colorado for vacation this summer. Is it much like Colorado?"

"*Is it much like Colorado?*" mimicked one of the mean boys sitting in front of Parker in a shrilly, high voice.

"Sounded just like her, Ivan!" the boy Grace had referred to earlier as Jeb whispered with an obnoxious laugh.

The smile on Grace's face wavered, but she turned to Parker, waiting for his answer.

"I mean... they both look very different from here," Parker said slowly. "Wyoming and Colorado have mountains."

"Oh, I just love mountains!"

Grace seemed like she was about to speak further when the bell rang loudly, and she waved good-naturedly, slipping into her seat in the front row.

The class had a simple, introductory lesson. Mr. Granger explained the importance of science and biology, among other things. When the teacher asked questions, Grace frequently raised her hand to answer, and seemed to quickly earn the teacher's respect. Meanwhile, Parker remained quiet the whole time, still feeling out of place. Perhaps he would have talked more if the two boys hadn't kept whispering so much and twisting in their chairs to glance at him. As much as they gawked, one would think Parker had two heads.

Eventually, the class ended, and students rushed out of the room with great speed. Parker fumbled with his schedule, looking for his next class, and entered the new room. Grace wasn't in this one, but neither were the two boys, so there was some relief.

Later that day, Parker learned that he had algebra with Grace, and literature with Jeb. Thankfully, other than biology, he shared no other classes with the other boy, Ivan.

Grace had been the only student to talk to him that day, other than the two who mocked him. Parker was relieved when the final class's lesson ended, and he hopped into his dad's pickup truck. It was a sleek vehicle, glittering black and adorned with a proud chrome grille guard.

"How was school?" Mr. Everson asked, pulling out of the parking lot.

"All right," Parker mumbled, staring out of the windshield at the distant woods and nearby farms.

"Make any new friends?"

"I don't know," Parker replied, looking down at his plain, black backpack. "One student talked to me. I think the others don't feel like they need any new friends."

"Well, did you try to introduce yourself?" Mr. Everson asked.

"No…" Parker admitted with a blush. "Since they've lived here their whole lives, don't you think they should welcome *me*?"

It didn't seem fair that he should have to push out of his comfort zone so much.

"Well, they should put in an effort," Mr. Everson agreed, stopping at a red light. "But that doesn't mean you shouldn't try to be friendly too."

"It seems some of them would rather talk *about* me than talk *to* me," Parker replied, shaking his head.

A flicker of disappointment flashed across Mr. Everson's face. They reached their new home before long, and Parker took in the sight of the house. It was considerably smaller than the one he'd lived in before. Personally, Parker didn't mind how big a house was, but he missed everything about his home in Wyoming. He missed the stillness of Wyoming nights, the bugle of elks, and the call of the coyotes. He missed ranch work and hiking among a million other things.

But most of all, he just missed the happiness of his family. That had disappeared well before leaving Wyoming, though.

Entering the house, Parker walked past the pile of cardboard moving boxes, still waiting to be unloaded. He dropped his backpack onto his bed, which had a very fluffy pillow and a navy-blue comforter. Looking around at the tiny space, he recalled the rustic, country look of his old bedroom. His new room was plain and dull in contrast. Of course, once all his stuff was unpacked, it would feel homier.

"When we get out of this rental and buy a permanent house," his father began, entering Parker's room, "we can buy some paint if you'd like. You've always said you'd like blue walls."

Parker thanked his dad, grabbed some scissors, and started cutting through the tape on the moving boxes by his desk.

He pulled out a western hat and hung it on one of the posts on his bedframe. Memories of helping his dad with cattle flooded his mind, but he blinked any threatening tears away. Mr. Everson had sold the cattle when they'd moved. The divorce had caused them to lose a lot of money, and now his dad was working as a hired hand instead of being the rancher himself.

Mr. Everson had cooked dinner while Parker had somewhat unpacked. As they sat down for the evening meal, Parker ate the simple bacon and eggs in silence.

"I know it's not as good as what Ramona used to make, but—"

"No Dad, it's fine," Parker interrupted hastily. "I like your cooking."

What he said was true. Personally, Parker didn't even want to talk or think about his mom right now. She hadn't seemed to consider him very much, anyway, so why should he allow himself the pain of remembering her? While his dad didn't cook as skillfully as his mom, at least his dad cared about him. That was more important.

"So," Mr. Everson began, changing the subject, "who was that student who introduced themself to you? You said one person had."

"Oh," Parker replied, "her name's Grace McClintock. She heard we lived in Wyoming and was telling me about how she's been to Colorado."

"I see. That's nice," Mr. Everson replied with a slight smile. Parker scarcely saw his dad smile anymore, and so he raised his eyebrows in surprise at the sight.

Continuing, Mr. Everson added, "See, maybe you're already making one friend. Now, if you introduce yourself, perhaps you'll make some more. You'll fit in in no time, Parker."

"I hope so," he responded uncertainly. "I felt so out of place today. It was like staring in a window of a house and watching everyone inside, seeing them talking and laughing. And all the while, I'm just beyond the walls, not being invited in."

*I've left Wyoming, yet I seem to have ended up nowhere,* Parker thought flatly. *How long will I be trapped in this empty divide?*

Life felt bleak. He wanted to go back to the world he'd left behind. He hoped to erase the memories of tears, fights, and disregard. He desired to live in years long since passed. It seemed it would be better to be caught up in a loop of happy days even if it meant never growing up, than to live in the present aches of loneliness. He felt that his entire existence was meaningless. Life seemed unfair and unkind.

But Parker pushed all these miserable thoughts away. He was sure his dad was feeling even worse than he was, so he needed to be there for him instead.

Parker asked his dad about the ranch he was working at. He was pleased the ranchers were at least kind and accommodating to Mr. Everson.

When dinner was over, Parker helped his dad

wash the dishes and put them away. He then retreated to his room to do homework, which didn't take too long since it was his first day of high school. He was sure the homework would get worse with time.

As Parker returned his books to his backpack, he couldn't help but reflect on the beginning events of freshman year. He had a feeling the two rude boys, Jeb and Ivan, weren't going to be pleasant company.

Parker was willing to at least try making friends with some of the other kids, since he knew his dad would want him to. If nothing else, he wanted to please his father. As he zipped up his backpack, he also wondered about Grace. She had seemed like a model pupil in their classes today, and she didn't appear snobby. On the contrary, she was warm, friendly, and *extremely* happy. Although not exactly popular among the students, Grace appeared liked by the teachers. Simply put, she seemed *good*.

Parker furrowed his brows in confusion. None of the other students at the school had even bothered to talk to him, but she had.

And there was something about her that he couldn't wrap his mind around. She seemed different, but for reasons he didn't know. Even if nothing had gone wrong in his life, he didn't think he'd be as nice and warm as Grace. What did she have that made her seem so good? Why was she so different from the other students he'd seen?

Parker didn't understand it. He wanted to feel

something besides the emptiness that settled inside his bones and wrapped around his heart. That void had formed since his mom became someone he hardly recognized. Not feeling anything was a very disturbing sensation.

Whatever Grace had that made her so different—so happy—he wanted.

# Grace's Faith

## Chapter 2

Entering school two days later, Parker introduced himself to several students. While some hardly paid him any notice, others were polite, but quickly turned back to their friends. At least he had tried though, so he figured his dad wouldn't be frustrated with him.

However, when he was exiting algebra class, Grace waved him down.

"Hi, Parker!" she said, looking as bright and full of life as ever. "I imagine it must be a big change, being in a new place. You haven't met my brother yet, right?"

"I don't think so," Parker replied. He didn't recall

any other students with the last name McClintock.

"He's a junior here," Grace explained, leading them through the hall, "so you don't share any classes with him. I was going to invite you to sit with my friends and me at lunch, but they're mostly girls. I figured that wouldn't be very fun for you! Perhaps you'd like to sit with my brother."

Recalling how he'd sat by himself the last two days, Parker nodded. It would be nice to not be alone while everyone else was in their groups.

A boy with blue eyes very much like Grace's, except they were framed in glasses, was pulling a textbook from his locker. He had black hair and a warm smile.

"Jacob!" Grace shouted cheerfully and waved at him. "Over here!"

The boy, apparently Jacob, shut his locker door and joined them.

"Jacob, this is Parker—he's from Wyoming. And Parker, this is my brother Jacob."

"It's nice to meet you," Jacob said with a smile, shaking Parker's hand. "What brings you to Ohio?"

Awkwardly, he explained hesitantly. "My parents got a divorce... Dad and I decided to move here because my grandparents are only an hour away... We wanted to be near family."

Jacob's eyes widened sympathetically.

Giving his condolences, he then said, "Well, I hope you'll feel at home here. I'm sure it's different, but maybe we can show you around the area sometime. I imagine you haven't been to the lake yet?"

Parker shook his head.

"Oh!" Grace piped up. "We should all go up then. We're going with our parents and Nana this weekend anyway, and it's not a very long drive anyway. Lake Erie's a lovely sight."

"Yeah," Jacob agreed, nodding enthusiastically. "So, would you like to join us? I know my parents won't mind us inviting you. If he'd like, your dad can come too."

Surprised that he'd already been invited to a get-together, Parker was taken aback slightly. Jacob and Grace genuinely seemed to want to be his friends. For the first time in what seemed ages, he felt excited, and a little less lonely.

"I'll ask if I can," Parker agreed. "It does sound fun."

* * *

Mr. Everson was going to have to work on the weekend the McClintocks invited them over. Though he was pleased people were making an effort to befriend his son, he was a little hesitant. Naturally, he was unsure about letting Parker go out with a family he, as the father, hadn't yet met.

"I don't think they're wild or anything, Dad," Parker reassured. "Their nana is coming, and Grace said her father's a *preacher*."

Mr. Everson nodded in thought, contemplating.

"I see. Do they know we're atheists?"

"Well, no…" Parker said slowly. Now he wondered if Mr. *McClintock* would approve of his own children's new friendship. "We're not wild either, though."

"I suppose it wouldn't hurt for you to hang out with your new friends," Mr. Everson decided, seeming to think they were safe enough. "Just because they believe in fairy tales doesn't mean you should stay home by yourself on a perfectly good weekend."

Parker thanked his father excitedly. It seemed the weekend couldn't arrive quickly enough. After all, he'd never been to any of the Great Lakes, and he figured this would be a fun opportunity.

He hardly even minded the teasing from Jeb and Ivan or that most of the students ignored his existence. Now he had something to look forward to, and a couple of people that wanted to know him better.

School seemed incredibly dull compared to the thoughts of going on a day trip with his new friends. Really, Jacob and Grace were just plain fun to be around. They always seemed upbeat—so free of drama or hidden motives. What you saw was what you got. To Parker, their presence was like a breath of fresh air.

Eventually, Saturday arrived. The McClintocks

pulled up to the Eversons' house in their large, forest-green van. It reminded Parker of a gigantic bug, but not in a bad way.

Hoping the McClintocks didn't mind that his house was rather small, Parker tried to recall if he'd mentioned it was only a rental.

"You must be Parker!" Mr. McClintock exclaimed. "I'm Cliff. The kids have been talking about you a lot lately—all good things, don't worry. This is my wife, Katie."

Mrs. McClintock looked as if she wanted to give Parker a warm hug, which startled him. He wasn't too used to hugs. However, she only gave him a polite, soft handshake.

"I'm excited to have you join us, Parker," she told him. "Have you been to any of the Great Lakes before?"

He shook his head and was about to reply when a small woman with a mixture of gray and red hair came to him.

"I'm Gwendolyn Agnew—Katie's mom, and Jacob and Grace's nana. Welcome to Ohio!" she exclaimed warmly. "Do you like exploring? There's a lot of sights to see."

"I do like to explore," Parker confirmed. "I used to hike in the mountains with my dad…"

"Good, good!" Gwendolyn Agnew cheered. "Now also, I know we're in northern Ohio, but have you ever had Cincinnati chili?"

"No, I think my grandparents might have?"

"Katie, we've got to introduce this boy to some, and soon!"

As Parker wondered what Cincinnati chili was, they clambered into the large van. Mr. and Mrs. McClintock were in the front, Grace and her nana in the middle row, and Parker and Jacob in the back. Thankfully, during the semi-long drive, Parker realized he didn't have to wrack his brain to think of conversation starters; the McClintocks and Mrs. Agnew had plenty of questions. Even though Parker was usually a quiet person, he found Jacob and Grace's family easy to talk to.

"Do you like camping, Parker?" Mr. McClintock asked.

"Mm, marshmallows!" piped up Jacob.

With a slight laugh, Parker answered, "Yes, I do—especially if there are s'mores involved. I used to go tent camping in the mountains when I was younger, but we also had a campfire ring at my old house, so we'd roast marshmallows on the property, too."

The memories of those old, happy days long gone sent a brief pang through his heart, but he pushed it aside. Today was going to be a fun day, and he wasn't going to let the past spoil it.

"You've never truly had a s'more," began Grace, turning around to face Parker in her seat, "until you've added peanut butter to the combination."

"Peanut butter?" Parker asked, with a tilt of his head. "I can see that being good."

"Yes! Sometimes I think it'd be fun to live in a different time period," Grace said, seeming to change the conversation. "But then I recall how there's no evidence peanut butter existed until recently. I don't think I'd enjoy living in a world without peanut butter half so much as one with it."

Parker couldn't help but laugh at this remark, even if he knew there were moments he wished he lived in a different time himself. Yet, he only longed to visit a decade earlier—back to when his family had been perfectly happy.

However, he wasn't going to ruin Grace's cheerful statement with such gloomy comments.

Jacob began talking about the careful, delicate efforts one must make to roast a marshmallow to its golden-brown perfection. The drive seemed to go by quickly, with everyone having a good time.

"There's the lake, up there," Mrs. Agnew said suddenly, pointing beyond the windshield. "Do you see it? It'll be easier to view when we're away from all these buildings."

Parker caught his breath. He'd only seen a glimpse of the blueness, but it was certainly beautiful.

Before long, Mr. McClintock parked the van, and the lake was now fully visible. As Parker stepped out of the vehicle, he was amazed at the sheer size of the lake.

"Over there is Canada," Mrs. Katie McClintock said, pointing to the very faint shoreline on the other end of the lake.

A couple of sailboats were sailing lazily across the water. Seagulls flapped their wings, soaring overhead. The gentle breeze and warm sunshine of summer's last days mixed to provide a purely blissful afternoon.

"I like looking at the ripples in the water," Jacob said. "We've been here just before storms, and the waves are really chaotic."

He picked up a smooth, flat stone, and flung it out to the water, watching as it skipped three times before finally sinking.

Parker reached for a similar rock and landed a couple of skips. The two boys soon made a competition of it, keeping count. However, Parker hadn't expected Mrs. Agnew to join in on the fun and out-skip them both!

"I wish I had Nana's throwing arm," Grace said with a laugh. She wasn't playing with them, instead just watching.

Mrs. Agnew began showing Parker her special technique, and he beamed when he began out-skipping Jacob. He was still no match for her, though! For a good half of an hour the three competed, and Parker couldn't recall laughing so freely in such a long time.

"I'm so thankful God made Lake Erie," Grace said when her nana and the boys finished their game and joined her and her parents.

It didn't make sense to Parker that the McClintocks felt a need to attribute all the things in the world to God. Besides, Grace was fifteen—he thought she should have learned to have more mature views by now.

"I'm thankful too, Grace," Mr. McClintock said. "He's made a beautiful world for humanity to enjoy. It was amazing seeing mountains on our Colorado trip. From the fossils within them, the global flood which happened so long ago still leaves its mark."

Recalling what he'd heard about the worldwide flood before, Parker looked away awkwardly. He was sure it was just another one of the fairy tales people believed in. But he didn't want to say anything to hurt his new friends' feelings.

*Even though He doesn't exist, it can't hurt them to believe in God,* Parker thought simply. *False hope isn't for me, but I guess it provides them with some comfort.*

"I'd love to become a paleontologist!" Grace chirped.

"Imagine digging up *dinosaur* fossils," Jacob replied. "At least we can still learn about the creatures of the past through their bones."

Entering the conversation, Parker said, "I've always liked t-rexes." He was glad to have something he could talk about with the McClintocks. Of course, he was sure dinosaurs used to live before, and felt it was a shame they were extinct.

With a jovial air, Jacob said, "I've always marveled at how Adam named all the different animals in the world, and yet I can barely remember what I ate for lunch yesterday."

Even though he didn't believe in Adam, Parker couldn't help but laugh at Jacob's remark. However, he was relieved when the topic changed from God, the creation, and the global flood to other things which he could become involved in.

After spending more time at the lake, they climbed back into the van. Parker found himself staring out of his window at the tall trees that formed endless woods. His dad had rightly described the forests as peaceful. Every time the nature occasionally dwindled, being replaced with cities and an abundance of houses, Parker felt a little dismayed.

"My next treatment is the Friday after this one," he heard Mrs. Agnew say to her daughter, dragging him out of his thoughts.

"How long is the chemotherapy supposed to last this time, Nana?" Jacob asked, concern visibly written over his face.

*Mrs. Agnew has cancer?* thought Parker, startled and feeling as if someone had punched him roughly in the ribs. He hardly heard her reply.

Parker saw Grace reach over and pat her nana on the shoulder gently.

"We're always praying for you," she confirmed softly.

Parker's heart wrenched. Now he knew with certainty that the McClintocks had troubles too. Yet... somehow they were still joyous. It didn't make sense to him.

But of course, they thought there was such a thing as a God that existed and heard their prayers.

Thinking to himself, Parker wondered, *What's it going to take for them to realize that He isn't real?*

# Evolution versus Creation

## Chapter 3

A couple of weeks had passed since Parker went with the McClintocks to Lake Erie. Ohio was still very new to him, and he was sure it was going to take a long time until he'd fully adjust. But at least the boxes in his room were now completely unpacked, and the house was starting to look more like a home.

In Wyoming, the cities are few. Parker's family lived about forty-five minutes from the nearest grocery store. As some like to put it, it seems most people in Wyoming live "out in the middle of nowhere."

To Parker, it was the only nowhere that felt like home. He was still trying to adjust to living in the suburbs now, as opposed to on six hundred acres. But their new home was only a rental anyway. He tried to content himself with the thought that one day they could get a ranch of their own again.

On the bright side, they had great neighbors. Mr. and Mrs. Walker, who lived next door, were elderly and therefore, unfortunately, didn't have any kids at home for Parker to befriend. But they were kind, friendly people, and Mrs. Walker had even made homemade strawberry jam for the Eversons as a housewarming gift.

The Walkers also had a big, fluffy German shepherd named Duke, and they let Parker visit him whenever he wanted to. Duke loved catching frisbees and was good company. Considering Parker had always wanted another dog, having one next door was the second-best thing. In the past, his family had owned an Australian shepherd.

When Parker had moved, he'd felt so upset that he thought he'd never be happy again. He didn't *want* to let himself be. Thankfully, by now, the cold, hard resentment pent up in Parker's heart had thawed and softened somewhat.

A couple of weeks ago, his father had asked him about how his visit with the McClintocks went.

Parker explained the fun they'd had, but left out the brief conversations about God and the flood and such. He didn't want his dad to think his new friends were too silly.

Sitting in Biology class again, he tried to keep his attention on the lesson. Of course, thoughts of playing catch with Duke filled his mind. Mr. and Mrs. Walker had invited the Eversons over for dinner that evening.

Parker and his dad had been taking turns cooking dinner each evening, and since this evening had been going to be Parker's night, he was glad to get a break. Unfortunately, the teen wasn't the best chef, and had burnt meals twice since they'd moved. He'd thought it would be nearly impossible to burn spaghetti, but somehow, he'd done it.

"For the rest of class today," Mr. Granger began, "we're going to be talking about the Big Bang theory. Does anyone care to explain what that is?"

One of the students in one of the middle rows raised her hand and, when prompted, said, "It's how the world began. Little particles formed atoms and expanded, making the universe."

"Correct, Sally," Mr. Granger said with a smile. "The universe is about fourteen billion years old."

Grace McClintock's hand shot up.

"Yes, Grace?"

"But it isn't truly a *theory*," she said, "because there isn't any real observable evidence for it, or that the universe is billions of years old."

Furrowing his eyebrows, Parker straightened in his seat. This was the first time he'd ever heard Grace disagree with a teacher.

"Well, of course there is evidence," Mr. Granger replied, flipping through the textbook calmly. "For example, there's carbon dating, which we use to find out the age of once-living things. We can look at fossils to see how long they've been around, which in turn, helps us find out how old the earth is. If we know the age of the world, we know the universe is even older. Of course, there's other things we use too."

"But carbon dating doesn't prove how old a fossil is. It's just a method which tries to guess," Grace explained. "Besides, how could there be fossils forming all throughout the years? Only a cataclysmic disaster could bury them so quickly that their bones were preserved."

"Well, what would you suggest caused the preservation of the fossil remains?" Mr. Granger said, seeming a little annoyed by having an apparent problem-student.

"The global flood," answered Grace promptly. "When God made the waters cover the whole earth, the mountains and the valleys changed. Mudslides and heavy sedimentation would have slid and the animals not in the ark were covered and died, being preserved from the quick burial. There are even remains of sea creatures found in the tops of mountains, which wouldn't be possible if it wasn't for the changing effects of worldwide flooding."

"A remarkable idea, Miss McClintock," Mr. Granger said. "Yet it has one flaw. God isn't real, and therefore, He never caused a global flood. Science doesn't support a divine force, because for something to be scientific, it must have been observed. Who can see God?"

"The Big Bang hasn't been seen," Grace replied. "And you can't say that evolution is just too slow to be observed either, because then you still have no proof. But there is plenty of evidence to suggest the world didn't form by random cha—"

"That is enough, Grace," Mr. Granger said sternly. "Let's return to the textbook."

Although Grace became silent, she looked as if she deeply wanted to say more. Parker didn't understand why she felt the need to disrupt the class. There was such a thing as taking a fairy tale *too* far, he was sure. Still, he couldn't help but realize she'd made a point when she said the Big Bang hadn't been observed. Was it therefore really science?

What's more, Parker knew Grace had been a favorite pupil of Mr. Granger's—at least up until now. It seemed strange that she would risk her teacher's favor over something Parker viewed so trivial. It didn't really matter how the world came into existence, did it? Parker figured the most important thing was that it existed *now*.

When class ended, Parker quickly gathered up his things to hurry to his next class. But he looked over his shoulder on his way out of the door in surprise, hearing Mr. Granger call Grace to stay behind.

"What exactly were you trying to prove in class today, Miss McClintock?" Mr. Granger asked.

Parker stilled, but quickly left before he could hear her reply, not wanting to be late for his upcoming class.

"Who would have thought the teacher's pet would bite back?" Jeb asked, opening a locker. "The look on Mr. Granger's face was priceless. Still, I wonder if she's going to get detention."

"I hope so," Ivan replied. "Having a model student in the room is pretty annoying."

Parker wished his locker wasn't so close to Jeb's and Ivan's. He didn't like having to hear their conversations, as they were usually about him. And even though he didn't agree with Grace, he didn't like hearing them gossiping about his friend behind her back.

Parker didn't have time to talk with her until algebra class. When he'd sat with Jacob and some other guys at lunch, he saw Grace, but she was on the other side of the cafeteria.

"Hey, why'd you do that in biology?" Parker asked as he arrived at algebra class, taking a seat behind her.

"Because although I respect Mr. Granger, what he said was wrong," Grace explained simply, turning to face him. "I couldn't just sit there."

"But how do you really know he's wrong about the Big Bang theory anyway?" Parker asked, surprised that Grace made such a bold statement.

"Why, because the Bible says God created the world in six days."

"Well, what if the Bible's wrong?"

Grace's mouth opened, but no words came out. Instead, she gave him a surprised look with her big blue eyes. Parker supposed she hadn't expected him to have such little faith—no faith, to be precise—in the Bible.

"Parker, don't you believe in God?" Grace asked at last, baffled.

"Well... no," Parker answered slowly, feeling his face grow hot. He wondered what Grace would think of him now.

*Maybe I shouldn't have brought anything up,* Parker considered to himself.

Before he had time to speak further, the bell rang shrilly, and he audibly sighed in relief. *Phew, just in time!* Now he wouldn't have to be confronted about his beliefs.

When class ended, Parker exited before Grace could talk to him.

*If I'm lucky, she'll just leave it at that,* Parker

thought. *Then by tomorrow it'll be long forgotten.*

But even as much as he hoped she'd forget; he wasn't sure *he* could put the thoughts behind himself. Why did Grace take her faith to such an extreme level? For what reason did she believe in God even when her nana was fighting cancer? Shouldn't her Lord have taken better care of her family? How could Grace believe there was a divine Creator when she'd never seen Him?

And how could Parker entertain the idea that something came from nothing?

* * *

It seemed the harder Parker tried to push his thoughts of biology class away, the stronger back they returned. He couldn't get Mr. Granger's and Grace's conversation out of his head.

*"A remarkable idea, Miss McClintock. Yet it has one flaw. God isn't real, and therefore, He never caused a global flood. Science doesn't support a divine force, because for something to be scientific, it must have been observed. Who can see God?"*

*"The Big Bang hasn't been seen. And you can't say that evolution is just too slow to be observed either, because then you still have no proof. But there is plenty of evidence to suggest the world didn't form by random cha—"*

What evidence had Grace been going to give before she was cut off? Although what she said about the Big Bang not being observed, and therefore not being science, was true, could there really be evidence to support divine creation?

As much as Parker didn't want to admit it, he knew Grace had been correct on at least one point where his teacher hadn't. And teachers were supposed to be the smartest people in the classrooms. So, did Grace know anything else that Mr. Granger didn't?

*But,* Parker mused, *Grace doesn't realize something. Even if, hypothetically, God does exist, then who created God? Or if He came from nothing, then why couldn't the Big Bang come from nothing too?*

This, Parker was sure, was a case Grace couldn't win, should she confront him. If he could prove that her faith had the same origin as atheism—something coming from nothing—then she wouldn't have a reason to think badly of his beliefs. Maybe she'd even agree with him.

Feeling invigorated by these thoughts, Parker walked toward the hall leading to his biology class the next day. He almost hoped Grace would bring something up.

"Hi, Parker!" Grace chirped from behind him, quickening her pace to catch up and shifting her lacy, denim backpack to her other shoulder. "You know that ice cream parlor I was telling you about? Jacob and I went there last night. We tried mint chocolate chip. That's your favorite flavor, isn't it?"

"Yeah," Parker replied, suddenly thinking that maybe he'd rather not have a confrontation after all. It would be nice to just push everything behind him and not rock the boat. "Was the mint chocolate chip good? I had one with some brownie bits added in before, when I lived in Wyoming. That was probably the best I've ever had."

Thoughts of Wyoming brought back bittersweet emotions. He tried to shove the memories of going to the ice cream parlor with his mom as a little boy away. Thinking about her wasn't pleasant. Part of him never wanted to remember her again.

"Our ice cream was great, but I think that addition would make it even tastier," Grace said cheerfully, walking at his side. "If I ever get to visit Wyoming, you'll have to give me the name of that shop."

"Yeah, absolutely. What's your favorite flavor, Grace?"

"Oh, strawberry! It's pink after all, and just so fun. Jacob loves rocky road. But you know him—he just adores marshmallows."

Parker laughed, recalling how the McClintocks had talked to him about camping and making s'mores before.

However, the happy thoughts died out when Jeb and Ivan walked by.

"Going to behave yourself today?" Ivan sneered, giving Grace a haughty look. "Or are you going act all high and mighty again?"

"I wasn't doing that," Grace replied softly.

Jeb tried to trip her, and then he and Ivan walked off, laughing loudly.

"They've been trying to trip me since the third grade," Grace said, brushing their actions off with a grin. "I'm so used to it that I know to look out."

"Have they ever succeeded?" Parker asked.

"No!" Grace answered with a giggle. "I think they should give up, don't you?"

"Mm-hmm," Parker agreed. Then, before he could stop himself, he blurted, "Grace, why don't you believe in the Big Bang, just because it's something coming from nothing? I mean, if God's real, something would have had to happen for Him to exist, right? If God created the universe, then who created God?"

He expected Grace to be astounded, but she merely smiled sweetly.

"Why, God's the creator of everything. He doesn't need to be created, because He's *always* existed. Some mindless particles floating around aren't divine. That's the difference. Divinity doesn't *need* to be created."

Parker fell silent, thinking quietly about what she said. She'd knocked the wind out of his sails, and he was trying to think of a rebuttal.

"But what if He doesn't really exist?"

Even as he said the words, Parker felt like it was

a lame response. Quickly, he added, "What's the evidence for a God? Maybe it's just that no one really knows how the universe came to be. How can you be so sure?"

"That's a good question," Grace replied as cheerfully as ever. "But there's a lot of evidence for God. There's *His* inspired word—the Bible—for one. It's so very long, yet none of the verses contradict each other, even though they were written by many, many inspired men. The Bible talks all about the creation of the world. And then, even without the Bible, you can see so much evidence in the world. There are the fossils in the ground, like we talked about before. The Bible speaks of a worldwide flood, and that explains how so many bones got persevered without decaying—even bones from marine life, which are buried in the tops of mountains."

The two turned into their biology classroom, and Grace added, "Also, by looking at how complex everything in the world is, from the plants and animals to the human body, one can see how there needed to be an intelligent designer. Everything's just way too complex to come about by pure chance."

Surprised, Parker thought over all of Grace's points. Even though he'd put her on the spot, she'd thought fast. Although he hated to admit it, she'd made an interesting argument. Obviously, Grace had put a lot of thought into these things before, which was something he couldn't exactly say for himself.

Soon, Mr. Granger entered and began the day's lesson, but Parker hardly listened to the class. He kept turning Grace's words over in his mind.

Any refutations he thought of were soon shot down in his own conscience, thinking of different responses Grace would almost surely make—worthy responses.

As much as he wanted to come up with a better argument for his case, nothing came to mind.

# An Invitation

## Chapter 4

Not one to give up easily, for the remainder of the day Parker mused over his talk with Grace. The rest of the week passed, and he was still thinking of it. Despite everything he wanted to believe, he did realize, deep down, that a divine Creator made more sense than some random particles expanding to make the universe. The Creator wouldn't *need* to be created, whereas particles can't exist on their own.

But after spinning his mind around in circles, searching for every argument he could think of, he'd thought of another question. He was convinced Grace would have a hard time grappling with this one.

To Parker, it had now turned into some type of a game to prove Grace wrong. If nothing else, he felt that changing Grace's mind would chase away any doubts within his own.

Unfortunately, there can be a sweet satisfaction in saying "I told you so," to someone. Although Parker liked the McClintocks, he still wanted to show them he could make an interesting argument for his beliefs—his beliefs being, of course, that God doesn't exist.

"Grace!" Parker shouted, spotting her in the hall on a sunny, late-autumn day.

"Hey! What's up?" she asked, looking like an innocent lamb—completely unaware of the thoughts Parker had been mediating on these last days.

"I've got another question about your God," Parker said triumphantly.

"Okay, try me!"

"If God's real, why does He let bad things happen? Why did my mom hurt my dad and me? And why did your nana get diagnosed with cancer? Since Mrs. Agnew worships Him, then He should protect her, right?"

Much to Parker's disappointment, Grace did not give him the sweet satisfaction he'd hoped for.

"That's a good question, Parker," Grace replied meekly. "The answer goes back to the beginning of time. When God created Adam and Eve, He took good care of them, giving them a garden which provided everything they needed. But Adam and Eve disobeyed His one commandment, which was not to eat fruit from one particular tree—the tree of the knowledge of good and evil."

She entered biology class and slipped into her desk, turning around to face Parker.

Continuing, Grace said, "As punishment, they were cast out of the Garden of Eden, and the world was cursed. Because of sin, death entered the world. That's why everyone dies eventually. Also, the wages of sin is spiritual death—separation from God because of our individual sin. You can read about all this stuff in Romans 5 and 6. Bad things happen in the world because of man's disobedience. While we didn't inherit Adam and Eve's sin—everyone bears the guilt of their *own* bad actions, like Ezekiel 18 says—the world changed when they disobeyed."

She paused, and then added, "More so, God has given us free will. He allows us to make our own decisions, and sometimes our decisions are sinful. But our actions *always* have consequences. I'm very sorry about what your mom did to you and your dad."

"But what's the point of it all?" Parker said aloud, thinking about the load of information Grace had just given him. "If God's real, why would He make us just for us to sin and then die. That doesn't sound very fun."

"If that was why He created humanity, you're right, Parker. It wouldn't be very fun," Grace agreed. "But we were made for a purpose. Those that repent of their sins and become Christians, remaining faithful to Him until death, will go to heaven when Jesus comes to judge the world."

Parker had to admit to himself that going to heaven after one's death would be a *lot* nicer than just dying and ceasing to exist. But his dad had said heaven was just a comforting fairy tale people told each other instead of accepting that they'd be nothing after death.

* * *

The possibility of God being real scared Parker. He was beginning to think that maybe trying to prove Grace wrong wasn't such a good idea. The more he tried to shake up her faith in the Creator, she met him head on with things he'd never even considered.

So, he ended the game. Parker tried to push all the thoughts away. Ignoring an idea makes it seem less real, anyway.

Instead, Parker slipped back into his routine. He went to school, did homework, and honed his cooking skills on scheduled nights. On Saturdays he spent time with his dad, or if Mr. Everson was working, visited the neighbors Mr. and Mrs. Walker and their dog, Duke. Sundays were spent sleeping in and sometimes going sightseeing with his dad, since Mr. Everson never had to work then.

Parker was still friends with the McClintocks, but he evaded all Biblical discussions. He hadn't made any other friends and was worried that the issue of faith might snap the ties holding his only two relationships together.

Besides, Parker contented himself with the notion that he was a relatively good guy. He stayed out of trouble, obeyed his dad, helped elderly Mrs. Walker get things off high kitchen shelves… He was a nice and polite fifteen-year-old after all. If God was real, Parker thought perhaps He'd be pleased enough with him and let him go to heaven, Christian or not.

He was beginning to adjust to life in Ohio. It wasn't the same as having mountains and six hundred acres with cattle, but he had to admit that exploring Mr. and Mrs. Walker's woods behind their house with Duke, and his own woods, was fun. Also, everyone in Parker's neighborhood seemed friendly, relaxed, and down-to-earth. Having nice neighbors was a big perk.

But Parker hadn't been expecting a phone call after dinner one Saturday evening—a call which would pull his routine right out from under him. It was the start of something that, yet again, would cause Parker to reflect on the past and think of the future.

When the phone chimed at full blast, Parker set down the pan he'd been drying and grabbed the phone seconds before it would cause the caller to leave a message.

"Hello?" Parker asked to whoever was on the other end of the line.

"Hey, bud! It's Jacob—what's up?"

"Just doing the dishes. What about you?"

"Not much. I was helping my dad with some mechanical stuff for our car," Jacob's voice came through the phone. "We were talking and wondered if you'd like to get together tomorrow."

"Oh, if my dad says it's okay, sure. Thanks for inviting me!" Parker responded, pleased at the unexpected offer. "What exactly were you thinking of us doing?"

"Well, would your dad like to come too? We wanted to invite you guys to come to church with us, and then come to the house after for lunch—my mom really wants to introduce you to Cincinnati chili."

Feeling a wave of nervous surprise at the invitation, Parker paused before replying. The McClintocks were trying to get him and his dad to come to church with them? At last, he said, "I'll... have to check with my dad."

"No worries, I'll wait here while you ask."

Parker could have almost laughed at how persistent Jacob was. Apparently, he was expecting him to talk to his dad about it right then. He set the phone down and went to the living room, where Mr. Everson was watching the news.

"Hey, Dad?"

"Hey, who was that on the phone?"

"My friend, Jacob McClintock, who I was telling you about," Parker answered, feeling hesitant. "Remember, I went to Lake Erie with his family?"

"Yeah, I remember. You had a really good time, didn't you?"

"Mm-hmm," Parker agreed. "Well, he wants to know if we'd join them for… church tomorrow, and lunch."

He felt a hot wave of embarrassment wash over him as his dad raised an eyebrow in surprise.

"Maybe you could say something like that you appreciate him asking, but we'll pass this time," Mr. Everson said.

Parker hadn't thought his dad would be very eager about the idea of going to church. Personally, Parker didn't really want to go either, as he figured it would just make him feel uncomfortable. But he wished he could spend some time over the weekend with the McClintocks again. It seemed like so long ago since they'd taken him to Lake Erie, and he felt happier than usual when he was with them.

"But we haven't got anything going on tomorrow," Parker replied slowly, then feeling really silly. He didn't want his dad to think he hoped to go to church with them. "It'd just be kind of nice to hang out with my friends again."

Although looking a little confused, Mr. Everson seemed to contemplate Parker's words. He probably didn't want to deny his son some time with friends when he was still trying to adjust to a new place.

"Well… I guess you could go… Would they be willing to pick you up?"

"Probably. I'll ask," Parker said, quickly turning to go grab the phone as his stomach somersaulted.

"Jacob?"

"Oh, hey Parker! Down for tomorrow?"

"My dad is just going to stay here, but he says I can go. Would you guys be willing to pick me up?"

No sooner had he said the words than he heard Jacob instantly say, "Sure! We'll be at your house at nine. If you need to borrow one of my ties, I can bring one over. Favorite color?"

Parker laughed at Jacob's enthusiastic response, all the while wondering what he'd just gotten himself into.

* * *

When Parker had left Wyoming, he'd never expected this. Here he was, riding in the back row of a big, green van, dressed in the best shirt and slacks he could find in his closest and borrowing Jacob's deep-blue tie. To be honest, Parker hadn't really known how to tie a tie, but his friend had helped with that.

Jacob and Grace's nana rode with them as well,

because the McClintocks always picked her up for church services. The McClintock men were wearing suits. Mrs. McClintock, Grace, and Mrs. Agnew wore bright, colorful dresses, which made them resemble the wildflowers in the ditch to the right of the road.

Parker had been a little surprised when he first saw his friends' nana, Gwendolyn Agnew, again. Concerned, he wondered how her cancer treatments were going, because she looked a little worn out. When he'd met her during their trip to Lake Erie, she'd appeared healthy despite her illness.

"I was very pleased when my grandson said you'd be coming, Parker," Gwendolyn explained, turning her head to see him from his seat by Jacob.

"Oh," Parker began, not really sure what to say, "thank you, Mrs. Agnew."

"Call me Gwen," she replied with a smirk that seemed to light up her whole face and push the weariness away.

"Thank you, Gwen," Parker replied, finding her radiating smile contagious.

Before long, they pulled into the parking lot. The McClintocks were early, and therefore, one of the first people to arrive.

Suddenly, Parker felt very nervous. He'd never gone to church before, and he didn't really know what to expect.

As they got out of the vehicle, Jacob gave his nana

his arm, in case she'd need help getting up the steps.

"Come on, Parker!" Grace chirped, her blue eyes shining. Grabbing him by the wrist, she gave him a gentle tug toward the church building. Clearly, Parker could tell she really loved going to these services.

As Grace dragged him toward the front steps, she whispered. "Don't be anxious, I think everyone's going to be very excited to see you."

"I don't know," Parker replied quietly. "I haven't ever been to a church."

"Oh, they'll be incredibly welcoming! We just love visitors," Grace chirped. "Now, we have a Bible class first, then everyone assembles afterward. I'll show you where to go!"

As soon as they entered through the front doors, they were greeted by two older men.

"Good morning, Grace!" one said, extending a hand for a shake. "Who's your friend?"

"Good morning, Mr. Mills! This is Parker Everson—mine and Jacob's friend from school!"

"It's nice to meet you, Parker, thanks for visiting today!"

The other man, Mr. Schneider, greeted them both and shook hands as well. Mr. Mills and Mr. Schneider's respective wives joined them too, warmly saying hello to Parker.

As Grace led Parker to a classroom in a hall, she said, "Those were the elders and their wives. Our

Bible class teacher is Oliver Rowland, and here's one of the spare lesson books—lesson seven's for today."

She also handed him a Bible on one of the desks. It had been with a few others, which apparently were for guests to borrow. From what Parker saw by looking through the lesson book, they'd be studying Job. He didn't know anything about that book of the Bible and didn't even recall ever hearing of it.

The teacher, Oliver Rowland, came into class a couple of minutes later. He was a tall, thin man with a set jaw and rectangular glasses.

"Hello there, who might you be?" Mr. Rowland asked.

"Parker Everson," Parker replied, shaking the hand that was extended to him.

"It's very nice to have you with us this morning," Mr. Rowland said. "Are you from around here?"

"My dad and I moved here from Wyoming," Parker politely replied. He wondered if he should mention this was his first time in a church but decided against it.

Before long, Jacob came in for class, as well as two other teenage boys and a girl.

One of the boys, named Ky, led a prayer, which Parker half listened to. He awkwardly looked down and closed his eyes like the others did but did not say "Amen." To Parker, prayer didn't mean anything.

First, Mr. Rowland gave some background

context on the book of Job for Parker's sake. Parker learned how Job was a wealthy man who'd lost everything—his children, his health, his friends, and yet he still obeyed God. The lesson recalled the thoughts Parker had been having before, about why God would let bad things happen to those who worship Him.

Even though Job had suffered greatly, he never stopped believing in God and doing His will. And in the end, God blessed Job significantly.

Jacob raised his hand, and Mr. Rowland called on him.

"Job shows," began Jacob, "that even when we have trials, they should strengthen our faith as we rely on God, instead of letting them cause doubt and anger."

The class went on for about forty-five minutes, and then they went to the auditorium for the worship service.

Many people greeted Parker, coming up to the pew where he sat with the McClintocks and Mrs. Agnew. Sandwiched between Jacob and Grace, he looked around curiously while everyone eventually took their seats. It was strange, seeing so many people preparing to worship a God Parker wasn't even convinced existed. What moved them to hold such a faith?

"Here, Parker," Mr. McClintock said softly,

passing him a Bible across the pew. "You can keep this one, no need to give it back."

He grasped the leatherbound, garnet-colored Bible. The edges of the pages were tinted gold, and it also had gold lettering on the cover saying: "Holy Bible."

One of the men stood at the podium and gave the order of announcements. After, Parker was surprised when Jacob rose from his seat and went up to lead everyone in singing hymns. There were no instruments—no piano, no organ… nothing! In between two songs, Parker leaned over to ask Grace why in a whisper.

"There isn't any biblical authority for it," she whispered quickly. Perhaps Parker didn't realize it was bad manners to talk, even quietly, during worship. "We're instructed to sing and make melody in our *hearts*—Ephesians 5:19. Words mean more than notes—they *praise*."

She said this last sentence with a smile, and began singing the next hymn happily with everyone else. Parker didn't join in, but he did listen to the words. Some hymns were loud, fast-paced, and full of gladness of heart. Others were slower, quieter, and solemn. And still others were things in-between.

The singing stopped, and a man led a prayer. Parker listened more attentively this time than he had in Bible class. The man thanked God for their ability to worship, for the visitors, for freedom, for salvation, and many other things. He also prayed for rulers in the world and for specific brethren that were sick or traveling. Parker liked that the man mentioned Mrs. Agnew, but he then caught himself wondering why he appreciated it. If God didn't exist, He wouldn't hear the prayer anyway. All this man's efforts would be in vain.

There was more singing followed by communion. Finding this especially intriguing, Parker listened intently. What was so important about some unleavened bread and grape juice?

He discovered that it represented the body and blood of God's Son, Jesus. Of course, Parker had heard of Jesus before. He knew people believed Christ came down from heaven and lived perfectly on earth. And he knew how they claimed He ultimately was sacrificed on the cross for every person ever. Those in the past, present, and—if the world remained—future, could be saved because of His death, burial, and resurrection. But if God didn't exist, then Jesus wasn't His Son, and it was all a big hoax.

Parker observed his friends partake of the elements. Jesus suffered and died, though He did no wrong. What a sobering thought!

After the Lord's supper, there was cheerful giving back of a portion of what the Lord had blessed the brethren with. Curious, Parker wondered what the point was. If God was real, He was in heaven and wouldn't need money. However, the speaker explained that it was for the work of the Christ's church: taking care of funds for the local congregation and helping brethren in need. Apparently, this church was helping support some preachers in other places. Parker watched as a couple of collection baskets were passed across the pews.

Then there was another hymn, and after it, Mr. McClintock stood up, going to the podium to deliver his sermon.

Parker listened somewhat, but at times his mind wandered to thoughts of home and school, or his eyes gazed out the windows. A cardinal hopped on a low tree branch. However, when it occurred to Parker that the McClintocks might discuss the sermon later, he shifted his focus back. It would be embarrassing to not know what they were talking about.

Mr. McClintock preached on submitting to God and trusting in Him. He turned to passages all throughout God's word and showed examples about different people in the Bible submitting and trusting in Him. But it was the example of Paul the apostle that stood out to Parker the most.

In Acts 9, Paul—then called Saul—had been persecuting Christians. He'd *felt* he was doing right, but that was all it was—a feeling. Sometimes feelings can be misleading. One day, while on the road to

Damascus, a light from heaven shone down and caused him to lose his sight. Saul was blind for three days and did not eat or drink anything. Eventually, a man named Ananias came to him and spoke to him. Then, the former persecutor submitted to God by obeying the gospel.

Then, Saul's name was changed to Paul, and he traveled far and wide bringing others to Christ. He was thrown in prison, stoned, beaten, and had many other terrible acts happen to him. Although he faced countless persecutions, he never forsook God, even when it ultimately cost him his life.

*People were willing to live and die for God,* thought Parker.

The teenager suddenly felt very optimistic. If God was real, maybe He could send a light down to prove it to him. Then he'd know what to believe for sure.

But then Mr. McClintock continued, almost as if reading his mind, by saying that the Lord doesn't perform such things today. People have God's word and can read the accounts of the miracles for themselves. Miracles ended a long time ago. No one should think they need a sign given before their eyes when they have the word of God in their hands. We are equipped with all we need.

Memories of biology class and his conversations with Grace flooded back to Parker's mind. Who was he to believe in the random chance of a Big Bang, when there was so much evidence in nature and elsewhere for a divine Creator?

Mr. McClintock's sermon had showed countless verses in the Bible all coming together perfectly. Those passages explained everything perfectly and without contradiction—even though the books hadn't all been written by the same author. They'd been penned by so many men over hundreds and hundreds of years! The reason there were no contradictions was because those words were inspired by God!

Parker saw there was evidence that the world was created for a purpose and not just because some random atoms expanded. Was the world really more than an accident? Was Parker's existence part of something bigger—something meaningful?

Mr. McClintock concluded that anyone who hadn't obeyed God wasn't His son or daughter. He said that they needed to put their stubborn pride aside and accept the truth, acting on it. Only then could they become a child of God. Parker's mind was caught on two passages, and he didn't hear the last parts of the message.

The passages he dwelt on were thus:

*Jesus said unto him, If thou canst believe, all things are possible to him that believeth.*

*In flaming fire taking vengeance on them that know not God, and that obey not the gospel of our*

*Lord Jesus Christ: Who shall be punished with everlasting destruction from the presence of the Lord, and from the glory of his power;*

The first passage was from Mark 9:23, and the next, 2 Thessalonians 1:8-9. Parker didn't like thinking about the everlasting destruction in 2 Thessalonians at all. If God was real, so was hell. And Parker couldn't avoid hell unless he chose to believe and obey.

The invitation song began, and then after there was a closing prayer. The service was over.

Parker wanted to get out of that church building and never come back. Surely, the word of God was piercing into his heart, and it was making him very uncomfortable.

God would take vengeance on those that didn't know Him.

Realizing what was happening, Parker was frightened. A horrible feeling of anxiousness swept over him. Quickly, he shoved his hands into his pockets, not wanting the McClintocks to notice that they were now suddenly slightly shaking.

Parker believed the universe hadn't come into existence through random chance. Evidence of an intelligent Designer—a divine Creator—was everywhere. Yes, Parker now fully believed in God. He believed, but he hadn't obeyed.

# Part 2

*Slowly I see the blessed truth*

*But my heart makes petty excuse*

*Though I know it's not a tale*

*I truly fear to cross the vale.*

# The Disdained Essay

## Chapter 5

God is real.

For fifteen years, Parker had lived his hopeless life ignoring his Creator's existence. Now, though, he'd realized the truth. It seemed to come on so suddenly. The truth frightened him.

There was something about being with the McClintocks that always made Parker feel strange. He felt... at home. Perhaps it was their welcoming, hospitable natures, or their binding family ties. They seemed to be everything a family should be, and that was something Parker hadn't experienced for most of his childhood.

Mr. McClintock was strong and sober, but not in a way that meant he never smiled. In reality, he smiled often. Something about the way he ruled his house—the involvement he showed and the radiating determination—impressed Parker. He'd seen nothing quite like it before, but he felt sure he himself wanted to be that way one day.

Mrs. McClintock treated Parker as if he was her own son. She was all he thought a mother should be. Yes, Katie McClintock was an abundance of things his own mom had never been. He'd seen few women who cared so deeply for those they loved. Her spirit was meek, yet extremely brave. She was tireless, devoted, and diligent.

Then there was the smart, studious Jacob. He was respectful and responsible and could quote verses off the top of his head as rapidly as a hunter plucked an arrow and shot it. Jacob was skillfully hitting spiritual targets with the word of God. Undoubtedly, he didn't do it for his own glory, but for the Lord's. Parker didn't feel that Jacob was ever trying to show off; he was only trying to spread God's word.

Grace's bright energy could light up any room. To her, all the simple joys of life, which so many overlooked, were pure pleasure. She herself brimmed with life. But Grace saw past all the flowers of the fields, past the forests… beyond dawn and dusk. Her heart and eyes rested on the hope of heaven, and Parker wondered if he'd ever see what she did. Grace could be incredibly sober when she wanted to.

And of course, how could anyone fail to mention Mrs. Gwendolyn Agnew? Although her physical body was growing weaker—though it was disease-ridden—her spirit was becoming stronger. Summing her up in one word was easy: righteous. In her presence, Parker felt as if someone understood him. Almost, he almost wished he was her grandson, and he hardly knew her!

Yes, this family had become a meaningful part of Parker's life very, very fast. They'd pushed him to think deeper about certain things than he ever had before, and it was overwhelming.

They'd helped him, even if their aid held a necessary sting. Because now Parker knew God existed, but that he wasn't serving Him. Are pain and anguish such terrible things when they are pushing one to further examine themself? For him, it certainly didn't *feel* good at the moment.

"What's the matter, Grace?" Parker asked with a surprised lift of his brows one early fall day. As he caught up with her in the school hall and they proceeded to algebra class, he noticed her latest essay in her hands.

Grace was reading the bright red ink on her paper, blue eyes larger than usual, her lips drawn tightly together in a firm line.

"Well, there's nothing wrong with me exactly," she whispered. "I've just received a terrible grade."

"Really?" Parker asked, leaning in to look. Sure enough, there was a big, crimson F on the paper, along with some feedback. This was surprising! How did she get an F? After all, he knew Grace was smart.

"Read it if you'd like," Grace replied, slipping the essay into his hand.

First, Parker observed Mr. Granger's response on the left corner, which said:

> *Miss McClintock, I asked you to explain the evidence for evolution, clearly not petty arguments against it. I trust you'll be more attentive next time, and wiser too. This grade is final and will contribute to your overall course percentage.*

Next, Parker read Grace's essay, which, sure enough, had nothing to do with the evidence for evolution. It ran thus:

> *Some say mankind is a mere animal, evolved over millions of years. Yet, where is the truth in that? If man came from apes, then why do apes still roam the earth? Or if humans and apes are supposed to share a common ancestor, then where is the*

*proof? When someone claims that bones form a "transitional fossil," they aren't showing reliable evidence. Instead, they are playing a guessing game. No one can prove that those bones formed some in-between creature. When has anyone ever seen one thing evolve into another? We try to cover up the inaccuracies by saying evolution is too gradual to observe. Well then, is it really science? No! Horses give birth to horses, and sheep to sheep, not anything else.*

*Man is not an animal. Rather, he was created in the image of God to have dominion over animals themselves (Genesis 1:27-28). Man's whole life—his whole divine purpose— centers on fearing God and keeping His commandments (Ecclesiastes 12:13).*

It went on further, but the bell rang, so Parker hastily gave the rejected essay back. However, it hadn't been disdained by *him*. He admired Grace for her courage. Not everyone was so willing to stand up for their beliefs. He himself wished he could say he'd done the same.

"It's good, Grace," Parker whispered as they slipped into their seats for algebra class.

She beamed at him so largely that Parker wondered if her face ached from it. To be honest, he hadn't exactly told her—or anyone—that he'd put aside his past beliefs. Admitting it was going to make it even more real, he knew. Wasn't changing his mind enough? Did he have to verbally express anything more?

Parker liked algebra. Apparently, he was a natural at it. Something about finding the secret number in all of those "x's" and "y's" was fun— almost like a game. It was certainly his most favorite subject. Often, Grace joked that Parker could surely do math in his sleep.

When class ended, he quickly gathered up his things and walked out of the door. Soon, Grace was right behind him.

"So," she began, "you liked my essay?"

"Mm-hmm," Parker replied, shoving a folder into his plain, black backpack as he walked. "I'm glad you stood up for your beliefs."

"And what did *you* write?" Grace asked, her bright blue eyes looking very intense and curious.

"I followed the assignment," Parker answered simply. "I wish I had been more like you, and written what I believed, though."

"I thought evolution *is* your belief," Grace replied with a tilt of her head. "The topic was evidence supporting evolution, anyway."

Feeling his cheeks heat, Parker shook his head.

Very quietly, he said, "No... I don't believe that anymore."

"Wait, really?" Grace asked, looking so happy one would think he'd told her he'd received a million dollars—no actually, she looked even happier than that.

Parker merely nodded, then gazed toward the door leading out of the school.

Shifting her lacy, denim backpack and pushing back a loose strand of hair from her messy bun, Grace said, "Well then, what do you believe now?"

For a moment, no words came out of Parker's mouth. Was he really going to express his views? Was he really going to make it this real?

Truth is worth voicing. There is no room for it to be merely quiet secrets. Perhaps Parker didn't quite understand that yet, but he knew he couldn't evade Grace's question.

"I believe God exists," Parker said slowly.

As for what else that meant, he didn't know. Simply believing in God is a very different thing than also obeying Him. Though he knew He existed, Parker hadn't yet committed his life to his Creator.

Letting out a gasp that sounded very delighted, Grace said, "Oh, *really*? I'm so excited to hear that! Since when?"

"Since I went to church with you guys," Parker explained awkwardly, at first looking down at his feet, but then bringing his gaze to her eyes. The truth was out. He'd just as well look her in the eyes, instead of avoiding her face like some shifty phony!

"That's wonderful!" Grace chirped. "What changed your mind?"

"A lot of things," Parker replied simply, stepping out into the fresh fall breeze.

By now, some of Ohio's tall trees were already beginning to array themselves in a myriad of colors.

Collecting his thoughts, Parker then added, "The things you've said—the evidence—about the world being more than chance really stuck with me. And your dad's sermon was powerful."

"Well, I'm really excited," Grace said. She looked like it, too. With a joyous smirk, she added, "You'd better come back to church with us again, Parker, okay?"

* * *

"You don't look well, Son," Mr. Everson said that evening. "Do you think you're coming down with something?"

"No, Dad," Parker answered plainly, staring down at his burnt dinner. Truthfully, he didn't believe he was coming down with anything except maybe a guilty conscience.

He'd been so caught up in his thoughts that he'd forgotten to take the casserole out of the oven. Uncomfortably, Parker wished he'd never learned the truth about God. To him, it was better to believe a lie than to have to deal with his fluttering heart and the butterflies in his stomach.

And he really didn't want to tell his loving father that he wasn't an atheist anymore. How would Mr. Everson handle the news? Would he be angry?

Placing his hand on Parker's forehead, Mr. Everson said, "I don't feel any fever. But maybe you should get to bed early today. Flu season's in full swing, you know."

Shaking his head vigorously, as if for nothing other than snapping himself out of his thoughts, Parker replied, "No, I'm fine. We're going to watch a movie, right?"

"Yeah, but it can wait," Mr. Everson said. "You don't look well. Maybe you should stay home from school tomorr—"

"I'm not sick, really," Parker interrupted firmly. "But I can go to bed early."

He really didn't want to skip school. Being home by himself all day while his dad was at work was always incredibly lonely for Parker. And he wasn't ill, anyway.

Reluctantly, Mr. Everson agreed. Of course, Parker was quick to change the subject. He didn't want his dad to change his mind.

"Did you like the sequel better than the original movie, Dad? I can't wait to watch the third one."

"I'm usually skeptical of sequels, but that one was pretty good," Mr. Everson answered, taking a bite of the casserole and kindly ignoring that it was burnt.

After dinner, as he'd agreed, Mr. Everson let Parker stay up for the movie. At least their popcorn wasn't charred. But once the credits rolled, Parker knew he was expected to go straight to bed.

Each day, enjoying life was growing harder. Parker's concentration on the film faded in and out. He only laughed slightly at a few comical scenes. Against his wishes, Mr. McClintock's sermon and Mark 9:23 kept flickering into his mind.

*Jesus said unto him, If thou canst believe, all things are possible to him that believeth.*

Narrowing his eyes, Parker thought to himself, *Well I believe! Isn't that enough?*

If this was what it felt like to believe, Parker wasn't sure he wanted to anymore. Since he knew fully well that God existed, he was uncomfortable all the time. Truth is truth, and nothing will change that.

Deep down, Parker knew he needed to do more than just believe in God.

He recalled hearing Jacob quote James 2:19 before, which said:

*Thou believest that there is one God; thou doest well: the devils also believe, and tremble.*

No, it was *not* enough to only believe.

Uneasily, Parker went to his room to retire for the night. The garnet-colored Bible that Mr. McClintock had given him was stashed away in his closet. He didn't know what his dad would say if he saw it, and Parker hadn't felt much like reading it. It had a way of stepping on his toes.

But it seems nothing keeps one awake better than a restless conscience. Parker truly felt miserable. For hours into the night, he tossed and turned. As he gazed blankly up at the ceiling, time flew away. Sleepless, he stared into the darkness toward the closest, which was illuminated by the moonlight slipping through the cracks in his blinds.

The verse which was imprinted in his mind the strongest wasn't Mark 9:23 or James 2:19. It was 2 Thessalonians 1:8-9.

*In flaming fire taking vengeance on them that know not God, and that obey not the gospel of our Lord Jesus Christ: Who shall be punished with everlasting destruction from the presence of the Lord, and from the glory of his power.*

Of course, he didn't want to be punished with everlasting destruction. But he had just enough hindering thoughts inside him to hold him back.

# A Persuasive Note

## Chapter 6

Days passed by, and with time, Parker felt less anxious. If he ignored them enough, Parker almost thought he could make his problems disappear. Nothing is further from the truth! If someone is grasping the edge of a cliff and denies they're in danger, does that change reality? Of course not. Yet minds have a way of playing tricks on us. We can believe just about anything we want to. And that is a horrible, frightening thing.

Hearing the phone ring loudly in the kitchen, Parker skidded in, finding his blue socks very slippery against the freshly mopped floor.

"Hello?" he asked, sliding into the counter with a

thump as he grabbed the phone and held it to his ear. In the living room, he saw his dad look up from reading a book on the couch.

"Hey, Parker!" piped up a voice through the phone speaker. "It's Grace."

"Oh, hey," Parker replied as he leaned against the counter, hoping she wasn't calling about what he worried she was. "What's up?"

"I just got home from shopping at the mall!" she giggled. "Do you want to come over tomorrow for church and lunch again? It's been a while. Your dad can come, too!"

Yep. She'd called for the exact reason he was afraid of.

Parker didn't intend to go back to church. He was sure that if he did, that guilty feeling in the pit of his stomach would resurface. It seemed easier to run away from his problems than to face them head on.

"Um, I think I'll pass this time," Parker said slowly. "Thanks for inviting me, though. Have a good weekend!"

"Oh," Grace said, audibly sounding disappointed. "Okay, take care."

Quickly hanging up, Parker then turned to retreat to his room.

"Who was that?"

Parker stopped halfway through the hall. He supposed he'd nearly gotten away unnoticed.

"Grace McClintock—from school," he replied

casually.

"What was she calling about?" Mr. Everson asked in mild interest, looking back down at his book.

"Oh… she asked if we wanted to go to church with them and have lunch after," Parker replied awkwardly. He wasn't an atheist anymore, but his dad was. And just because Parker believed in God, it didn't mean he was planning to do anything about it.

Before Mr. Everson could say anything further, Parker hurried to his room and shut the door, locking it. He sat down on the floor with his back against the door and sighed. He wanted to see his friends, and he hated hearing Grace sound so disappointed. But what could he do?

Life, as he'd thought before, seemed very unfair. He just couldn't explain why, though. Maybe it was because he felt very lonely now, sitting quietly in his room. Perhaps it was because his mother had never cared for him the way Katie McClintock cared for her children. Or possibly it was because Mr. McClintock was a preacher and had raised his kids in a happy home.

Maybe Parker just wanted the life his friends had.

They didn't seem overwhelmed by guilt. Instead of tossing and turning until two in the morning, his friends had some type of sweet assurance. And unfortunately, it was a comfort Parker was sure he could never claim.

Moving his eyes across the floor and to the other end of the room, his gaze slipped to the gap between his bed and the floor. His lips twisted into a frown as he mechanically reached for an object stashed away between the carpet and bedframe.

In his hands was a picture that brought overwhelming sadness into his heart every time he looked at it. It was a photograph from a decade ago—at his fifth birthday—and he was sitting on his mom's knee, both of his parents smiling happily. A picture which years prior had brought a smile now only brought a scowl.

*I'm nothing but a misplaced puzzle piece,* Parker told himself sulkily, anger beginning to bubble up in his chest. *I don't feel happy anywhere. Why did I even keep this?*

Frustrated, he jumped to his feet and thumped the framed photo into his small trash bin. He didn't ever want to see it again! It just made him think of all his many broken dreams.

There was a firm knock at the bedroom door.

"Parker?" Mr. Everson called through the locked entrance, likely having heard the thud. "Are you okay?"

"I just want to be alone…" Parker moaned back, voice cracking. He felt some strange type of irritation gripping him.

Just in time, he stopped himself from adding with a shout, "Go away!" He knew his dad only wanted to help him. And Mr. Everson had his own share of pain and problems.

Hearing his dad's footsteps trailing off, Parker figured he was respecting his son's wishes and reluctantly letting him sort through his own problems.

Parker clenched his teeth and tried to push away the miserable feeling that was suffocating him. But it doesn't work to push away one's own frustrations instead of dealing with them. Now that he was left to think, Parker wasn't sure he really wanted to be by himself after all.

In reality, he'd always hated being alone.

\* \* \*

Sunday was a bright, crisp day.

As was their custom, the Eversons had slept in. Eating a completely plain piece of toast, Parker noted the time on the clock, recalling how Jacob and Grace were studying Job in Bible class now. If he hadn't declined Grace's offer so quickly, he would have been with them, too.

But he wanted to stay as far away from church as possible. Parker decided he didn't have time to feel guilty. In a few years, he'd be graduating from high school, then off to college, and then out on his own. Life was too busy to start thinking about religion.

At least that's what he kept telling himself.

While he tried to convince himself that biking or taking a walk this morning was nicer than sitting in a "dusty old pew," he kept recalling his friends. He didn't want to admit it, but there seemed to be more meaning in spending the first day of the week in church than outside taking a Sunday stroll.

Mr. Everson was outside watering the trees, which he'd always found quite soothing. Since Parker was planning to help his dad, he finished his toast and then headed to his room to get his shoes on.

Ducking under the shelves in the closet, he reached for the simple black footwear and stood up.

"Ouch!"

He'd accidentally hit his head on one ledge. Catching sight of his cap shoved in a dark corner of the closest, he reached back and retrieved it. But while he did so, his fingers had brushed against something else.

Lingering at the wardrobe entry, Parker stared, his forehead creasing in thought. His hand had touched the Bible that Mr. McClintock had given him. To try to forget the divine words inside of it, he'd hidden it as far back into his closest as possible. But it was still there, waiting for him.

Without thinking, he reached for it and flipped through the different books. His memory had gotten the better of him, it seemed. He just *had* to read that one passage again, to see if he'd truly remembered it properly.

"2 Thessalonians 1..." he mumbled to himself under his breath as he tried to navigate the large

Bible. He was surprised he'd remembered the book and chapter of the passage.

Scanning over verses 8 and 9 a few times, he saw they still read the same as they always had.

*In flaming fire taking vengeance on them that know not God, and that obey not the gospel of our Lord Jesus Christ: Who shall be punished with everlasting destruction from the presence of the Lord, and from the glory of his power.*

Disappointed, he read the previous verses, trying to see if there was any further context. It did not make him feel one bit better. Although the earlier passages talked about good things, he knew those verses didn't apply to his present state.

Flipping through some more pages, he searched around to see what else the Bible's writers had to say. He stumbled upon 1 Timothy.

*Didn't Jacob mention something before about the apostle Paul writing letters to someone named Timothy?* Parker wondered to himself, trying to wrack his brain. He'd enjoyed hearing about Paul in Mr. McClintock's sermon that one time that he'd gone to church with them.

Skimming through the first chapter, his eyes read over verses 14 and 15 twice. Those two verses in particular really stood out to him.

*And the grace of our Lord was exceeding abundant with faith and love which is in Christ Jesus. This is a faithful saying, and worthy of all acceptation, that Christ Jesus came into the world to save sinners; of whom I am chief.*

Paul had turned his life around and been saved. Previously, he'd led an unrighteous life, yet he'd found hope. Surely there was hope for Parker too, then.

But a glance out of his window showed Parker that Mr. Everson wouldn't be watering the trees for much longer. Quickly, he slammed the Bible shut and stashed it into the back of his closest again. What would his dad say if he'd seen what he'd been reading?

* * *

Another month passed. Parker hadn't really read much more of the Bible since that Sunday when he'd passed up the McClintocks' offer to go to church. He'd convinced himself it was all too overwhelming and that it just wasn't worth it. For some odd reason, he wanted his life to stay the same. He was tired of change.

Although Jacob and Grace were as friendly to him as ever, they hadn't brought up him coming with them to church again. Deep down, Parker couldn't tell if he was relieved or disappointed. In the past, when his friends had tried to say things, he'd changed the subject. They'd probably gotten a clue that he didn't enjoy talking about his beliefs. Parker wondered if his friends were finally going to leave things alone.

This week, Grace had missed a couple of days of school. Unfortunately, she'd caught a rather troublesome head cold—a sign of the cooler weather that had settled in. Now, on Friday, she'd returned at last, and was like her usual, bubbly self. Of course, she still sounded a little congested, but that would resolve itself in time.

Today was a test day for algebra class. Parker was feeling confident about the exam. Even though he probably hadn't needed to, he'd spent an extra half hour studying last night.

"I really hope there are some true or false questions on this test," a front row student muttered to his friend. "You've got a fifty percent chance of being right!"

"Or you could just use common sense instead of writing in an answer before you even read the question," one of the other students, this time from the middle row, retorted with a tremendous eye roll. "Why don't you just pay attention to the lectures for once?"

The teacher entered which silenced any further remarks. For Parker, the test was as easy as ever, and he zoomed through the problems with plenty of time remaining. In case he'd possibly made a mistake somewhere down the line, he looked back through his work.

The satisfaction of a good grade in algebra made up for the rude remarks he'd had to put up with from Jeb in literature class earlier that day. It would be nice if Grace was in literature with him, to balance out the unpleasantness of Jeb's presence. But Parker wouldn't wish the pain of sharing another class with the mean boy on anyone.

After the bell rang, the students' papers were turned in, and Parker happily left the room.

"Hey, wait up!" Grace chirped, dodging students as she sprinted to him. Her nose was still red from her cold, but her eyes were their usual vivid, life-filled blue.

"What's got you in such a rush?" Parker laughed, turning to head to his locker before he left the school.

"Oh, I've got to get home and help Mom with housecleaning," Grace explained. "So unfortunately, I haven't got any time to talk. But I *have* this. See you later, Parker. Bye!"

She pressed something into his hand before she pushed back through the myriad of students, soon lost from sight.

Lifting an eyebrow, Parker saw she'd given him a note. Quickly, he unfolded it and then read over it several times, surprised. In Grace's neat, cheerful handwriting, it read:

*Hey! If you aren't obeying God, you aren't right with Him. What's holding you back, Parker? Talk to me about it. Okay?*

There was a little smiley face drawn at the end of the message. Staring at the paper in his hands, Parker almost found himself smiling—almost. Apparently, Grace wouldn't let him evade the nagging thoughts that now always swirled in the back of his mind.

# Push Back

## Chapter 7

That weekend, Mr. Everson had to work, so Parker was home alone. While most teens loved Saturdays, Parker hated them if his dad was gone. They seemed to go by so terribly slow.

To escape the solitude, he often paid the next-door neighbors a visit. Considering Mr. and Mrs. Walker had long since retired, they were usually home. On the occasion that they were gone too, Saturdays were incredibly frustrating.

Knocking on the door, Parker waited for one of his elderly neighbors to answer.

"Parker! How nice of you to visit," Mrs. Walker exclaimed, inviting him inside. "Do you want to play with Duke?"

"Sure. Here, these are for you," Parker replied, handing her a small plate of chocolate chip cookies. "I hope they taste all right. My baking skills are improving, I think!"

"Oh, I'm sure they'll taste especially good," Mrs. Walker reassured with a smile. "Thank you, dear."

The home smelled of melting wax. A large, cranberry scented candle was on the fireplace mantle, glowing serenely against the honey-colored wall.

Parker loved the Walkers' house. It was incredibly cozy, with plush couches that had thick, crocheted blankets thrown over the backs. Often, the fireplace was crackling merrily. Family photos covered the walls. Mr. and Mrs. Walker's children and grandchildren no longer lived in Ohio, but plenty of pictures were displayed of them. Clearly, family was constantly in the Walkers' thoughts. Parker wondered if his own mom ever thought of him. Since she'd hardly considered him when she was with him, he doubted anything had changed.

"How's Christopher?" Mrs. Walker asked, snapping Parker out of his troublesome thoughts.

"Dad's good," he answered. "He had to work today though, so I thought maybe I could drop in."

"Well, you know I meant it when I said you are always welcome to come over," Mrs. Walker told him pleasantly. "All of my grandchildren are in either Arizona or Massachusetts now. Grandmas get lonely too."

Mr. Walker was seated in his recliner reading a newspaper, but he removed his reading glasses when Parker entered the living room. Duke was at the kind old man's feet, and the German shepherd lifted his head and let out an enthusiastic bark.

"Look, Norman," Mrs. Walker told her husband. "Parker's brought us some cookies."

"Well, thank you," Mr. Walker said cheerfully, reaching for one of the treats, and taking a large bite. "Mm, you've really outdone yourself, Parker! I think this is your best batch."

Parker grinned broadly. His practice was paying off!

*I've successfully baked a batch of cookies, and I didn't even burn the house down in the process,* Parker humorously thought to himself.

Mrs. Walker went into another room, and returning, she now had a frisbee in hand.

"Now here you go," she said with a smile.

Taking the frisbee, Parker went out through the backdoor with Duke. The big German shepherd had a fierce personality when he didn't know someone. But any friend of Mr. and Mrs. Walker was a friend of Duke's. The animal loved Parker.

"Okay, you ready?" Parker asked with a smirk to the eager dog. "Catch!"

The frisbee soared toward the woods, and Duke darted off, leaping into the air and catching it before it landed on the ground.

Parker lavishly praised the dog and gave him a good scratching behind the ears. His dad used to have an Australian shepherd that did herding on their ranch, but that was a few years ago. For a long time, Parker had missed having a dog around.

In the crisp, late-fall air, he played with Duke for a good hour, playing catch, exploring the woods, and jumping into piles of leaves. Perhaps some would think it immature for a fifteen-year-old to be jumping into leaves, but Parker didn't see any harm in it. Eventually, he and Duke returned to the Walker's home, and they were feeling very thirsty. Duke panted loudly with his tongue sticking out lopsidedly.

"I hope I didn't tire your dog out too much," Parker told the Walkers with a light laugh, filling a glass of water for himself at the sink.

"Not at all," Mrs. Walker responded cheerfully. "If anything, he's got too much energy and needs a teenager such as yourself to help him let it out."

"Come and take a load off, Parker," Mr. Walker invited, motioning to an empty seat on the couch.

When Parker sat down on the plush couch, Mrs. Walker offered to make hot chocolate. Leaving to do so, she hummed as she entered the kitchen.

"Now," Mr. Walker began as he turned down the volume of their small, old-fashioned television set, "how was that algebra test you had?"

"Really good, thanks," Parker answered, recalling the proud, bright-red ink that had marked the top. "I nearly got a perfect score—I just missed one step on one problem, you know how that is."

They talked about it for a while until Mrs. Walker returned with three steaming cups of cocoa. Quickly, Parker rose to help, since it was a lot to carry.

"Hey, I've actually got a question," Parker said as he sat back down, sipping the sweet, warm drink.

"Fire away," Mr. Walker said with a good-natured chuckle. "And Lily, this hot chocolate is good, as always."

Looking Mr. Walker straight in the eyes, Parker asked, "What do you think someone has to do to be saved?"

Parker figured that since his neighbors were old, perhaps they'd be the wisest people to ask. He didn't know a lot about their religious background, but they attended church somewhere, he recalled. Although he hadn't talked to Grace about salvation yet, he figured he might ask on Monday.

"Well now," Mr. Walker began, setting his mug of cocoa down on the coffee table, "you believe in God, right?"

"Yeah," Parker said.

"I'd imagine John 3:16 would answer your question," Mr. Walker replied pleasantly.

"What's that say?" Parker asked, blushing. He hadn't told the Walkers that he was raised by atheists.

Of course, the fact he was just now wondering what someone needed to do to be saved might have been a telling sign.

Mrs. Walker grabbed the large Bible they left opened on their coffee table. It was in good shape, which perhaps suggested it was used more as decoration than anything else.

"We have it opened right here, dear," she said, placing the Bible in Parker's lap.

He found the sixteenth verse of the third chapter and read over it a couple of times. Suddenly, Parker felt very relieved.

*For God so loved the world, that he gave his only begotten Son, that whosoever believeth in him should not perish, but have everlasting life.*

"So, if I believe in Him, then I'm saved?" Parker asked. He thought that seemed easy enough.

Nodding, Mr. Walker said, "That's right. Believe and God will save you!"

"But wait," Parker said, suddenly recalling something as he bit his lip. "What about that one verse? The one that says something about devils—or demons—believing? Are they going to be saved, too?"

"I think that's in James, isn't it?" asked Mrs. Walker, taking the Bible from Parker and turning for a look. After a moment, she said, "Oh yes, here it is,

James 2:19. It says, *Thou believest that there is one God; thou doest well: the devils also believe, and tremble.*"

Mr. Walker gently took the Bible from his wife's hands, and flipped through the stiff, crisp pages.

"John 3:16 is talking about good people who believe and accept Jesus into their heart," he said simply. "Whereas James 2:19 is referring to those who believe but are bad people. If you believe and want to make God happy, you're fine."

"Okay..." Parker said slowly. He guessed that made enough sense.

After his talk with the Walkers, Parker felt better than he had in a long time. He contented himself with the thought that since he didn't dislike God or anything, he was going to go to heaven one day. Shouldn't salvation be relatively easy to obtain?

\* \* \*

Monday rolled around quickly, and Parker once again made his way to school.

"Hey, Grace!" he shouted across the hall on the way to algebra class.

"What's up?" Grace asked, turning around with a big smile. "Have an answer for that note I left you?"

"Yep!" Parker affirmed. Triumphantly, he declared proudly, "It turns out, I'm already saved!"

"What do you mean?" Grace replied with a tilt of her head. She seemed confused.

"Well, I believe in God, don't I?" Parker

questioned with a grin. "And I'm a decent person. John 3:16 says that if you believe in God you won't perish, but that you'll live eternally."

"Yes, it does," Grace agreed, which only made Parker's grin grow. "Believing is part of the picture, for sure, but it isn't the whole thing."

She'd more than just rained on his parade—she'd blown everything away!

"What do you mean?" Parker replied. He said it more like a statement than a question. In his heart, Parker felt annoyed that Grace disagreed with him. Here he'd thought she was going to be excited for him! He was offended.

"Well, you've got to look at the Bible in its entire context," Grace explained. "Like James 2—"

"I already know about that," Parker interrupted, recalling what Mrs. Walker had said. "Of course, someone can believe but still be lost. That's only if they hate God, like the demons."

"Is that what the Bible says, Parker?" Grace asked, her big blue eyes looking at him with incredible seriousness.

Falling silent, Parker reflected. He felt that deep down his own statements hadn't really made sense.

"For example," Grace began, "John 12:42-43 shows that you have to be willing to *confess. Nevertheless among the chief rulers also many believed on him; but because of the Pharisees they did not confess him, lest they should be put out of the synagogue: For they loved the praise of men more than the praise of God.* The chief rulers believed, but they didn't want to openly commit to serving Christ. Now, also in Acts—"

The bell rang, and whatever Grace was about to say was lost in the commotion. The class started, but Parker had never had such a troublesome time focusing on his favorite school subject! He knew Grace had shown him a passage that debunked the views that he'd just previously held. Sure, he'd told her he believed in God before, but that didn't exactly mean he wanted to let other people know about his new views. He really didn't want to tell his dad. So, he was like the Pharisees in John 12.

What other truths had Grace been about to bring to light?

He didn't know, but he felt incredibly gloomy. For a short amount of time, he'd thought he'd been saved! Now, however, he realized he still wasn't. What Mr. and Mrs. Walker had told him was simply not true, despite their good intentions. After algebra class, Grace tried to continue their conversation, but Parker left abruptly. He didn't want to hear anything more, because he had a feeling whatever she said was going to prove one thing:

Obeying God would cost Parker something.

* * *

For a few weeks, Parker evaded the McClintocks. He was worried they'd try to talk to him about salvation, and he absolutely did *not* want to deal with that. He kept telling himself it was just too hard.

But clearly, ignoring one's problems does not make them disappear. Parker still had a lot to learn.

Eventually, though, he became very lonesome and missed his friends. Other than his dad and the Walkers, he didn't have anyone to talk to or hang out with. And despite the nice company all three people were, they couldn't fill the void of having friends his own age to relate to.

At long last, Parker couldn't stand it any longer. He felt very foolish for pushing the McClintocks away when they'd only ever been kind to him.

"Jacob! Grace!" Parker called, hurrying to them just before they exited the school's doors.

"Hey, what's new with you?" Jacob asked, holding his hand out for a high-five.

"Not much, really," Parker answered, slapping his friend's palm. "But it's been too long. I'm sorry, guys."

"We should catch up," Grace said simply, though she smiled perhaps a little too big for her casual tone of voice. "I'm going to talk to Mom about having you over for dinner."

Surprised, Parker hastily said, "Oh, you don't have to—"

"Nonsense!" Grace chirped cheerfully. "Now would you come if we ask you? Are you free this week?"

"What day?" Parker asked.

"Probably tomorrow."

"Grace!" Jacob exclaimed in astonishment at her response. "Are you trying to send Mom to an early grave?"

"Of course not," Grace replied, humorously sticking her nose up in the air in a dignified manner. "I'll help Mom prepare everything. It's been too long since we've all gotten together."

Since the next day was Thursday, Parker almost sighed in relief. He figured it would be safe enough to accept Grace's invitation, if her mother said it was all right for him to come. She wasn't trying to get him to visit on a Sunday or anything when he knew he'd be "roped into" going to church.

"I should be free then," Parker agreed, beaming. "But only if Mrs. McClintock says it's okay."

With a laugh, Jacob said, "You know how she feels about you calling her that."

"Okay, if *Katie* says it's okay, I'll come."

"Great!" Grace cheered. "Well, we'll call and let you know if it works out or not. Bye!"

Parker never guessed the next day would forever change his life.

# The Decision

## Chapter 8

Regardless of the short notice, Katie McClintock had put together a feast surprisingly fast. Of course, Grace had helped every step of the way. But it was amazing what a couple of pairs of hands could accomplish in such a quick amount of time.

When Parker arrived, he was welcomed by the aroma of something savory. It took him a moment to recognize the scent until he realized it was the smell of meatloaf. Recalling that he'd mentioned to Jacob before how much he loved meatloaf, Parker smiled to himself. Mrs. McClintock was clearly trying her best to make him feel at home.

With fond memories, he recalled when the McClintocks had had him over for lunch on that fateful Sunday all those weeks ago. Back then, they'd had homemade Cincinnati chili, and it was certainly unlike any chili he'd ever had before. It rested on a bed of noodles, but despite its unusual presentation, it was truly delicious. Aside from topping the chili with cheese and some oyster crackers, one could use different garnishes such as onions, kidney beans, and hot sauce.

Today, Mr. McClintock—or Cliff, since he preferred Parker to call him by his first name—had picked him up. Jacob had also joined them. (Unfortunately, Parker's dad, although invited, didn't come.)

Every time Parker walked into the McClintock family's home, he couldn't help but grin. They lived in a two-story house with light-colored walls—Grace had said the paint was labeled, "Alpaca," and it gave off fresh, cozy, inviting vibes. The floors were wooden, and the kitchen countertops were made of marble, which was very aesthetically pleasing.

But it was more than the appearance of the house which made him feel at ease. The people inside it were the most important part. They were what kept the house feeling like a home.

"Good evening, Parker," came a voice from a rocking chair positioned near the fireplace. "It's a pleasant time for knitting."

It was Gwendolyn Agnew, or Gwen. Parker held back a gasp when he saw her. As it had been a long time since he'd last seen her, he hadn't realized how frail she'd become since the last time he saw her. She looked as if she were wasting away, and his heart wrenched inside his chest.

Her smile was still as vibrant as ever, yet her eyes revealed some of her masked pain.

"Gwen," Parker said, coming toward her as she knitted. "It's been too long."

"It certainly has," she replied sadly, and the familiar twinkle in her eyes sparkled out. For a split second, she almost looked well. "Katie thought I'd like to join you guys tonight. I'm lucky; it's not every day I get to see Parker Everson!"

Mrs. Agnew could make anyone feel appreciated. Parker hated to see her looking so helpless and in pain.

"Can I get you anything?" Parker asked, looking around.

"No, no, I'm just having a little fun," she answered, holding up her knitting project. "I'm hoping to get this sweater done soon."

It was a sweater made of thick wool and colored a deep, deep blue.

"It sounds like Grace is coming down," Gwen said with a soft sigh. "My Granddaughter's quite the knitter herself, but as soon as she and Katie got the dinner finished, she went up to take care of Tabitha."

"Tabitha?" asked Parker.

Mrs. Agnew tilted her head toward the stairs.

At this moment, Grace came bounding down the steps with a big, soft, cuddly tabby cat in her arms. As it meowed enthusiastically, the cat was perhaps the perkiest and happiest cat that Parker had ever seen.

"Hi, Nana, hi, Parker!" Grace piped up, sliding across the wooden floor in her pink socks, which had little stars on them. Her hair was thrown into its usual messy bun, and her eyes were a kind of blue that even the sweater couldn't compare to.

"Hey, Grace," Parker replied. "I take it this is Tabitha?"

"Mm-hmm, want to hold her?" Grace asked, pushing her arms toward him before he could even reply. "She's always wanting attention!"

Taking Tabitha, he found her to be a truly loveable feline. He'd never petted a cat with such a silky coat before, or held one that was so playful yet gentle.

Mrs. McClintock announced it was time for dinner, and so Parker didn't get to hold Tabitha for long. She purred and rubbed against his legs. Carefully, Grace helped Gwen up from the rocking chair and to the kitchen. Mrs. Agnew was slow to her feet and her teeth clenched, revealing a grimace of pain. Although Grace was cheerful, as always, Parker could tell she was concerned for her nana. He was a little concerned about her as well.

Jacob led the prayer. It was quite the meal. There was meatloaf and mashed potatoes and green beans and beets, followed by a delicious pumpkin pie. (Grace had made the pumpkin pie herself, since it was apparently her specialty. Anyone who had it could confirm it was fantastic.)

Throughout the meal, Katie kept on trying to make sure Parker had enough water, asked if he needed any dish passed, and checked on other such things that a host worries over. Clearly, Parker was taken good care of.

After the meal, Jacob went to retrieve a board game. Apparently, there was a new one he'd received for his birthday, which the whole family enjoyed, and they wanted to introduce it to their friend.

While Katie and Grace cleared away the things in the kitchen and shooed everyone out, telling them to go relax, Parker went with Mrs. Agnew.

"Are you feeling okay?" he asked in a small voice.

"That depends on how you look at it," Mrs. Agnew replied with a smile as she settled down into her rocking chair.

"What do you mean, Gwen?" Parker asked with a tilt of his head, pulling a chair up by the fire for himself.

"Physically, I'm tired and aching," she replied softly. "But spiritually, I'm refreshed and soothed.

Yes, in Christ I feel truly alive."

"I don't know what that's like," Parker slipped out, before he could stop himself. "I guess I'm only feeling fine physically."

"What's holding you back, Parker?" Mrs. Agnew asked, looking at him with her intelligent, curious eyes. Surely, Grace had inherited her own bright blue irises from her.

"I don't know," Parker said simply.

"Well, time's running out," Gwendolyn Agnew stated. "No one knows when their life will end. Of course, I'm sure that mine's ending soon. I'm seventy."

She did not say this last sentence with a look of disappointment, but rather a fond smile.

As Parker didn't know how to reply, there was silence for a moment. He wanted to tell her that she'd get better and live for years and years, but his mouth opened only for no words to tumble out. Then, Mrs. Agnew said, "Go on. What's troubling you? Why are you waiting to be saved?"

Parker thought long, staring into the flames of the fire. Why was he delaying? He knew he hadn't fulfilled God's will. What was holding him back from getting right with the Lord? At last, he muttered decidedly, "I'm afraid to commit."

Gwendolyn turned to Parker. "And what do you think you'd rather have? Yielding to your good, peaceable, loving Creator, or living your life with no real fulfillment, only to die and face judgment with regret?"

Parker gulped, and Mrs. Agnew waited for him to reply. Inwardly, he knew the answer.

Jacob returned with the board game, and Mrs. McClintock and Grace entered the living room also. Grace picked up Tabitha and sat on the floor near the fireplace, cuddling the cat. Tabitha seemed quite pleased with the attention.

Parker looked down at his hands, running through his thoughts in his head. At last, he said, almost to no one in particular, "But how is a person saved?"

He vaguely remembered Mr. McClintock talking about it in his sermon before, but he wanted to make sure he fully understood.

"That's a great question, Parker," Cliff said, joining the conversation. He reached for his worn-out Bible, which had often-turned pages and verses underlined in pencil. Flipping through calmly, he said, "Well, first you have to listen—to hear the word—right?"

"Yes," Parker agreed quietly.

"Romans 10:17 says, *So then faith cometh by hearing, and hearing by the word of God.* Of course, hearing is simply not enough. You must also believe—have faith."

"I like John 8:24," Jacob said, then quoting, "*I*

*said therefore unto you, that ye shall die in your sins: for if ye believe not that I am he, ye shall die in your sins.*"

"Well, I do believe," Parker insisted.

"Very good!" Mr. McClintock praised. "Do you think that's enough?"

"I don't know… Well, no, I suppose not," Parker confessed, recalling his conversation with Grace from a few weeks ago.

"You're right," Cliff said. "If you want to be saved, you can't go on living in sin. What do you think of Acts 17:30-31?"

The evangelist turned there, and passed the Bible to Parker. Reading over it, the teen read the passage.

*And the times of this ignorance God winked at; but now commandeth all men every where to repent: Because he hath appointed a day, in the which he will judge the world in righteousness by that man whom he hath ordained; whereof he hath given assurance unto all men, in that he hath raised him from the dead.*

"It says you're commanded to repent," Parker responded slowly, feeling uncomfortable. "Repenting is regretting your wrong ways and turning from them, isn't it?" He hadn't truly done that. For example, although not very often, he'd sometimes told lies.

"You're absolutely correct. Instead, we're

supposed to replace our bad things with good things," Mr. McClintock confirmed. "Parker, Jesus came to earth to die on the cross as a sacrifice for our sins. He died for every single person. He died for you. And He rose from the dead and ascended back into heaven. The Bible says He's coming back one day, to judge the world."

Clearing his throat, Mr. McClintock continued. "Now, one can't just repent and go on hiding their faith. Turn to Romans 10, if you will, and read the ninth and tenth verses."

Parker did. It read thus:

*That if thou shalt confess with thy mouth the Lord Jesus, and shalt believe in thine heart that God hath raised him from the dead, thou shalt be saved.*

Parker thought about all this very carefully.

"Now, Parker, there's one more step to becoming a Christian, and we don't want to overlook it and do injustice to God's word," Mr. McClintock said. "Will you turn to 1 Peter 3:18-21?"

Parker did, though he had a little trouble finding it. After all, he wasn't used to using a Bible. Reading the passage, he saw it said:

*For Christ also hath once suffered for sins, the*

*just for the unjust, that he might bring us to God, being put to death in the flesh, but quickened by the Spirit: By which also he went and preached unto the spirits in prison; Which sometime were disobedient, when once the longsuffering of God waited in the days of Noah, while the ark was a preparing, wherein few, that is, eight souls were saved by water. The like figure whereunto even baptism doth also now save us (not the putting away of the filth of the flesh, but the answer of a good conscience toward God,) by the resurrection of Jesus Christ.*

"We know Noah built the ark to save his family from the flood that destroyed the whole world. Baptism, by the resurrection of Jesus Christ, saves us like the waters saved Noah from a sinful world," Mr. McClintock explained. "Christ was buried, and when one's baptized, their old, sinful man is also buried, though in the waters of baptism. They resurrect out of the watery grave as a new man, pure like Christ because they've obtained salvation from their sins. Romans 6:4 says, *Therefore we are buried with him by baptism into death: that like as Christ was raised up from the dead by the glory of the Father, even so we also should walk in newness of life.*"

Parker was following, albeit slowly. He didn't have a lot of knowledge about the Bible, but this made perfect sense to him. God's plan isn't complicated.

But gloomily, Parker knew he hadn't obeyed His plan.

"Keep in mind, Parker, that there are a lot more verses about each of these points. You can't leave out even one part of the plan of salvation and expect to be saved. How about we look at another example of a person who obeyed the gospel? This time, turn to Acts 8."

Parker read over the chapter, seeing it was about a eunuch that hadn't yet obeyed the gospel, and how a man named Phillip converted him. He read over verses 35-38 twice.

*Then Philip opened his mouth, and began at the same scripture, and preached unto him Jesus. And as they went on their way, they came unto a certain water: and the eunuch said, See, here is water; what doth hinder me to be baptized? And Philip said, If thou believest with all thine heart, thou mayest. And he answered and said, I believe that Jesus Christ is the Son of God. And he commanded the chariot to stand still: and they went down both into the water, both Philip and the eunuch; and he baptized him.*

It suddenly became crystal clear to Parker. Phillip had preached Jesus to the man. Preaching Jesus *also* meant preaching belief, confession, and baptism. Someone who hasn't believed, confessed, and been baptized doesn't have Jesus. It is that simple and easy.

If Parker wanted to be saved, he knew what he had to do. He had to be saved like the eunuch. The eunuch hadn't delayed a moment! There was just one thing Parker wasn't sure about yet.

He tilted his head. "But what if you mess up after you become a Christian?"

"You repent and ask for forgiveness," Mr. McClintock answered simply. "As 1 John 1:9 says: *If we confess our sins, he is faithful and just to forgive us our sins, and to cleanse us from all unrighteousness.*"

The truth stood before Parker plainly. If he wanted to be saved, he couldn't sit around and do nothing. He wasn't right with God. Although his dad might be upset, it didn't change the Lord's pure word. He *had* to do what was right, no matter what anyone else thought. Seeing Mrs. Agnew physically wasting away yet spiritually thriving, Parker realized all the genuine joy and peace of being right with the Lord and having hope in heaven.

And he realized that rejecting God for one's own earthly pleasure was a horrible mistake that would affect that person for all eternity. He couldn't even fathom the infiniteness of forever—of the never-ending.

God had created mankind, and therefore Parker, with a purpose. He had sent Jesus to die for every person. The Holy Spirit had been with the apostles as they wrote the inspired word that showed these things. Parker had read that word, and he understood what he was required to do.

All his life he'd felt alone. But with God, he'd never be abandoned. Truly, the Lord was good, just, and... and *perfect*! At last, Parker realized how silly he'd been. Why had he tried to resist? The Lord was wonderful, and Parker now realized, wholeheartedly, that he *wanted* to obey and worship Him!

Parker Everson was willing to put away his faults. He wanted to change and have his sins washed away. And no matter the cost, he fully wanted to profess Jesus. He wanted to be saved.

"Mr. McClintock," Parker said suddenly, rising from his chair in haste. "I need you to baptize me."

# Part 3

*The waters wash away my sin*

*Now I start life fresh again*

*Yet Satan wants my soul, he schemes*

*To take my precious faith from me.*

# The Change

## Chapter 9

O n the drive to the church building, Parker felt like he was dreaming. At last, he'd put away all his foolish, stubborn pride and was he going to be saved!

In the big, green van, he said with a laugh, "Pinch me, Jacob. Ouch! Yep, definitely awake."

Staring out at the streetlights shining in the darkness, Parker watched the buildings as they whizzed past. Since it was well after rush hour, the streets weren't too busy.

Currently, Parker was trying to stop shaking. Although mostly from excitement, he was feeling very nervous.

The drive didn't take long. When they arrived, everyone piled out of the vehicle in an instant, and Mr. McClintock went to unlock the front door of the church building.

Holding the door opened for them, Cliff flicked the lights on.

It had been so long since Parker had last walked into this building, and the familiar appearance brought a wave of sweet nostalgia. So much had changed since his last visit!

Cliff showed Parker a small room which had nylon baptismal garments and such, and then left to get himself ready, shutting the door.

In the background, Parker could hear Jacob was leading hymns in the auditorium. They were sweet, blissful songs of faith and salvation!

Heart thumping so loud that he could hardly hear the hymns, Parker, now clad in the water-repellent garment, opened the door that led to the baptistry.

A song finished. Cliff McClintock was already standing on the other end of the baptistry, dressed in some overall waders.

"Parker," he said, "do you believe that Jesus Christ is the Son of God?"

"Yes, I absolutely believe that Jesus is the Son of God," Parker replied firmly. He believed with his whole heart, and what a wonderful feeling it was to no longer strive to resist!

"Then I baptize you in the name of the Father, the

Son, and the Holy Spirit."

This was it!

Recalling that in the van Grace had suggested he hold his nose when baptized, ("So no water goes up!") he quickly did so. Mr. McClintock took him and dunked him in the water. Swiftly, he lifted Parker back up, and neither could stop smiling. Parker Everson was a Christian—he had obeyed the gospel found in the New Testament!

"When you rest your head on your pillow tonight," Mr. McClintock said, "think about how good it is to go to sleep in full confidence that you're God's child. As Galatians 3 says, *For ye are all the children of God by faith in Christ Jesus. For as many of you as have been baptized into Christ have put on Christ.*"

He patted Parker on the shoulder happily, and they exited the baptistry to return to their small rooms. Jacob resumed leading hymns. Filled with pure peace, Parker prayed to God, his heart full of thanksgiving. He'd never prayed before, but he realized how comforting it was to have a Lord that would listen.

When Parker entered the auditorium, he joined in the singing and slipped next to Grace in the front pew.

After the hymn ended, Jacob came and clapped him heartily on the back, exclaiming, "Now we're not only friends; we're also brothers in Christ!"

Everyone was giving him hugs and congratulations. In all his fifteen years of life, Parker had never felt so joyous.

Grace pressed a note in his hand, smiling so big that her face surely ached. He could not yet look at it, there was so much going on. But that was why she'd written her words down; he could read what she had to say later, when he got the chance.

Mrs. Agnew looked less pained and ill; she was filled with such gladness. Everyone chattered excitedly for a long time. They talked about Parker's conversion, different Biblical topics, and other such things. It was truly the best day of Parker's life.

Unfortunately, the night was growing late, and they eventually had to leave and drive Parker home. He felt nervous at the idea of telling his dad about his new faith, but he knew he'd made a commitment to Christ. If his dad was upset, that wasn't going to change Parker's mind that he'd done the right thing.

Before leaving the building, Mr. McClintock led a prayer. Then, with a clean conscience because of his obedience to God, Parker entered the van. His heart felt incredibly light.

"If you need a ride," began Mr. McClintock as he started the engine, "we'll pick you up Sunday morning for worship!"

"Thank you, Cliff," Parker said gratefully. "And thanks for having me over for dinner, guys. I had no idea that I'd finally accept and obey the truth today.

My only regret is that I fought against it for so long."

The night sky was cloudless and bright with innumerable stars. Snow blanketed the ground. The van arrived at his house, and Cliff parked. The McClintocks (and Mrs. Agnew) didn't drive off until they saw Parker unlock the front door of his home and enter inside.

The house was silent, and all was dim. Mr. Everson was in his room, probably about to go to sleep, but had heard the door.

"Parker?" he called from his room. "Did you have a nice time?"

"Yes, Dad," Parker said.

He was trying to think of where to start first, when Mr. Everson said, "Good. I'm called out to work early tomorrow, so I'm off to bed. Tomorrow we'll talk about your visit, okay?"

"Oh," Parker said surprisedly, realizing he'd have to postpone the somewhat nerve-racking discussion. "Okay. Goodnight, Dad."

Absentmindedly, Parker walked to the kitchen and pulled a milk jug out of the fridge. Pouring himself a glass, he leaned against the counter, thinking about everything that had happened.

He pondered how simple and holy God's plan of salvation was. It made perfect sense! It wasn't enough to do one part and ignore another. Each aspect lined up together to bring about a change in one's heart. When somebody believes in God and wants to serve Him, of course, they will repent of their sinful behavior. They will want to profess their Lord and be washed in the waters of baptism, raised to walk in newness of life. Like Romans 6:4 says, the old man is then buried in the watery grave.

Finishing his glass and rinsing it, Parker left the kitchen. As excited and good as he felt, Parker wasn't sure he'd be able to sleep for a while. Entering his room, he turned on a small lamp and flopped down on his bed.

With his mind full of the delight of the night, he pulled Grace's note out of his pocket. Unfolding it, he read:

> *Hey! I'm writing this as we're in the van, driving to the church building for your baptism. I'm really very overjoyed, and I hope that you'll serve God all the days of your life! Here are a couple of my favorite verses. Keep them in your heart:*
>
> *"Therefore if any man be in Christ, he is a new creature: old things are passed away; behold, all things are become new." (2 Corinthians 5:17)*
>
> *"Fear none of those things which thou shalt suffer: behold, the devil shall cast some of you into prison,*

*that ye may be tried; and ye shall have tribulation ten days: be thou faithful unto death, and I will give thee a crown of life." (Revelation 2:10)*

*No matter what afflictions come, Christians can endure them—even if that trial is death—because they've put on Christ. Don't ever forget that!*

Good, sweet, righteous Grace! Parker smiled at the note, thankful to have made such a friend as her. Now that he reflected on his life, he realized how glad he truly was to have moved, for it was in Ohio that he'd learned the truth of God. Maybe he'd left many precious things behind, but he couldn't help thinking of all the deep, meaningful things he'd come to now obtain.

In the past, his life had been miserable. Now he lived with a purpose. He lived for Christ.

\* \* \*

"Dad," Parker began, "I need to talk to you."

Slowly inhaling, he attempted to steady his shaking hands. Parker was trying to remind himself that it didn't matter what anyone thought of him, as long as he was right with God.

*What's Dad going to think about me...?* Parker wondered frantically, feeling the suffocating pressure grip him. It was one of the worst feelings he'd ever experienced. How was Parker going to get the words out that were stuck in his throat?

The world could disown him, but he was a Christian.

"What is it, Son?" Mr. Everson asked. Because of the urgent look on Parker's face, he took a seat on the couch and muted the television.

Parker sat down next to him. His heart throbbed in his chest.

"I…" he trailed, looking his dad straight in the eyes. "I believe in God."

A long, horribly awkward pause.

"You're joking."

"No," Parker replied firmly. "I'm serious! Dad, He *has* to exist. There's so much evidence. Oh Dad, He sent His Son to die for the world. He—"

"Believing in God is believing in a fairy tale," Mr. Everson said promptly. "Son, don't tell me those friends of yours have influenced you to trust fiction? I thought I raised you better than this…"

Christopher Everson looked deeply saddened and worried. Parker hated disappointing his dad. But there was nothing to be done. He had to do the right thing, whether his dad agreed or not.

"He's *real*, just let me talk to you about it!" Parker pleaded. "I'm… I'm a Christian now."

"Since when?" Mr. Everson asked, raising an eyebrow.

"Since last night," Parker answered. "I repented, confessed, and was baptized."

With a slight shake of his head, Mr. Everson stated, "Parker, you can't believe these things. Heaven's just a story people made up so everyone wouldn't be so sad when their loved ones die."

"Dad, what's the meaning of life?" Parker asked rhetorically.

"There isn't any really," Mr. Everson responded. "I guess life means whatever you want it to mean."

"No," Parker said. He jumped up, ran out of the room, and retrieved his Bible from his closet.

He'd bookmarked the page he had in mind the night before, ready to show his father in the morning.

"Look here," Parker said. "Ecclesiastes 12:13 says, *Let us hear the conclusion of the whole matter: Fear God, and keep his commandments: for this is the whole duty of man.* That's the meaning of life, Dad."

Mr. Everson let out a long sigh. "But the Bible isn't true. God doesn't exist, and heaven isn't real."

"And why doesn't He exist?" Parker questioned.

"Because faith in God isn't science."

"Faith in evolution isn't science either," Parker pushed. "Were you there when the universe formed? No man's observed the creation of the world, therefore the way it formed can't be scientific fact. But God gave us the Bible, which explains the creation of the universe. *He* was there when He made it, so He *has* observed it. Plus, I've seen that the Bible agrees with science, whereas evolution doesn't."

"That's ridiculous!"

"No, it's not," Parker replied quickly. "The Bible lines up with science. Evolution claims that one thing evolves into another over a long period—so long that no one can *observe* it. People must have been able to observe something for it to be science. Nobody's ever seen one kind of creation become another. But the Bible teaches that God created everything to reproduce after its own kind. Yes, there are different breeds of dogs for example, but they're all still *dogs*! We can observe that dogs always give birth to dogs, not cats."

"Well, what about the transitional fossils?"

"You can piece old bones together and try to visualize them as something else, but that doesn't actually prove that they were some in-between creature, now does it?" Parker queried. "Bones only reveal so much. There hasn't been any difference in the fossil record.

"How do you know?" Mr. Everson said, looking his son straight in the eyes.

"Well, for example, I was reading an article a few weeks ago, and I saw that there were fossils of a creature that was thought to be extinct. It turns out that coelacanths have been discovered again, and there is no change. It hasn't evolved or anything. If things are evolving, how come coelacanths are the same as before? Shouldn't they have changed?"

Parker was amazed at how quickly he

remembered the things he'd heard and read, when he had to say them fast. Unfortunately, it was impossible for him to read the expression on his father's face. Was he beginning to understand?

"I've got to get to work."

Parker's heart sank. His dad had just ignored everything he'd said.

"Dad," he began. "Let me leave you with one more thing."

"… Okay," Mr. Everson relented, looking at his watch as he stood up to grab a cup of coffee.

"I'm going to read Psalm 33:4-9 for you," Parker explained, turning quickly to the passage. "It says, *For the word of the Lord is right; and all his works are done in truth. He loveth righteousness and judgment: the earth is full of the goodness of the Lord. By the word of the Lord were the heavens made; and all the host of them by the breath of his mouth. He gathereth the waters of the sea together as an heap: he layeth up the depth in storehouses. Let all the earth fear the Lord: let all the inhabitants of the world stand in awe of him.* Dad, this is how we know the origin of the earth. Evolution can't tell us, but it's recorded here, in the Bible. God wants us to obey."

"I can't believe in God," Mr. Everson said, going into the garage. "If He's real, then He certainly hasn't treated me well, has he hmm? Don't you remember why we moved to Ohio?"

"Yeah, because of Mom," Parker answered. "But just because she hurt us, that doesn't make it God's fault! He gave us the ability to decide for ourselves, and sometimes those decisions hurt others. Mom made a sinful decision, but God cares for everyone. He wants us to do what's right!"

Mr. Everson didn't reply, just gave a stiff smile and waved as he got into his truck and left.

# God's Family

## Chapter 10

**"I**'m going to church, Dad," Parker said determinedly that Sunday morning, smoothing some gel into his light-brown hair.

"You don't want to spend my one day off this week with me?" asked Mr. Everson in surprise with a sad look in his eyes.

"It's not that I don't want to be with you," Parker explained, not liking the guilt trip. "I do want to spend today with you. Why don't you come to church with me?"

"I've been working all week," Mr. Everson replied. "I'm trying to relax for a while."

"Although worship takes effort, it's fulfilling," Parker responded, straightening his deep-blue tie in a mirror. Jacob had given it to him to keep. "Deep down, humanity longs to worship. Unfortunately, they just don't always worship Who they *should* be worshiping *how* He wants to be worshiped. I know I'm going to be very edified today."

*If you'd just accept the truth, Dad, you'd see that God is worthy of worship, and you'd see how comforting it is to give it to Him,* Parker thought, disappointed that Mr. Everson wouldn't even listen.

"I guess that's why people believe in fairy tales. It makes them feel better," Mr. Everson replied simply, turning on the news. Personally, Parker didn't think watching the news looked very pleasant or relaxing.

"It's not a fairy tale," he said, giving an exasperated sigh. Glancing at the clock, he realized the McClintocks would be here any minute. He'd better finish getting ready.

Heading to his room, Parker pulled his scarlet-colored Bible from his closet. Of course, he didn't shove it in the far back corner anymore. He wanted it to be only a quick reach away.

"Psalm 33:4-9, Dad," Parker called out as he opened the front door and exited. Giving a wave, he then shut the entrance and walked down the driveway. The large green van sparkled in the winter sunlight.

Snow crunching beneath his feet, Parker gave a couple of good stomps before jumping into the vehicle. He didn't want to bring the slush and ice into the McClintocks' van.

"Good morning, Parker!" everyone cheered.

"Hey guys," Parker responded, taking his usual seat next to Jacob. "How's it going?"

"We're good," Mrs. McClintock answered, turning around and giving him a warm smile. "Especially because of you! We're elated over your conversion."

"I am too," Parker said with a slight laugh. Then, feeling a grieved twist in his heart, he softly added, "I just wish my dad understood. He's not too happy with me."

"I'm sorry to hear that," Mr. McClintock replied, using his turn signal as he then entered another road. "We're praying for him though, and you. How about turning to Luke 12:51-53?"

Parker flipped through his Bible. It took him a moment to find the passage, but he knew that eventually he'd improve at locating the different books.

Finding it, he saw it said:

*Suppose ye that I am come to give peace on earth? I tell you, Nay; but rather division: For from henceforth there shall be five in one house divided, three against two, and two against three. The father shall be divided against the son, and the son against the father; the mother against the daughter, and the daughter against the mother; the mother in law against her daughter in law, and the daughter in law against her mother in law.*

"You've got to do the right thing," Cliff McClintock said, "even if no one agrees. So, keep on doing good, and don't let it weary you."

"Galatians 6:9," Jacob added with a smile.

Intrigued, Parker turned there too. It read:

*And let us not be weary in well doing: for in due season we shall reap, if we faint not.*

"I see," Parker replied. "Thanks! Dad and I are going to my grandparents for Thanksgiving, and I don't think they're going to be enthusiastic about my choice either... So, prayers for that would be appreciated too, guys."

Obeying God can be hard, but it's worth it. No one should expect that the narrow road is easy. It means putting aside our own worldly desires, and also even, when necessary, our own family ties. God is a Christian's Father, and Jesus, a Christian's Brother. It is better to serve God and be saved, than to elevate your loved ones above Him and be lost.

As they drove, Parker longed for a family like the McClintocks. But now, he and they were both part of

God's family. Although not physically his relatives, he knew they'd do anything to help him in his walk with the Lord.

Arriving at the church building, everyone climbed out of the van.

"Come on!" Grace giggled. "We already told the brethren about your conversion. I'm sure they're just *dying* to see you again."

Of course, they were. When he entered, the elders—Mr. Mills and Mr. Schneider—were the first to welcome him, as well as their respective wives. There were a *lot* of greetings and congratulations, and Parker blushed, not used to having so many people talking to him at once and such. But it was a warm, wonderful feeling, knowing that there were people that truly cared and supported him in his new faith.

When Parker reached Bible class, he was happy to see they were still studying Job. He'd thought it seemed like a very interesting book, even if he didn't understand all the context just yet. In time, things would become clearer. After all, he'd spent fifteen years not going to church or reading a Bible. There was a lot to learn.

Unlike the other time that Parker had attended church, he now focused and participated. Usually, he wasn't one to sing *ever*, but he did join in now, as hymns are a part of worship, and therefore important.

Mr. McClintock got up to deliver the sermon.

Sitting cheerfully next to Parker, Grace was taking notes with her pink pen and turquoise notebook. Jacob wasn't taking notes, but he was turning to every passage as quickly as he could.

When Mr. McClintock revealed the topic of the lesson, Parker smiled to himself a little. It was a lesson on life after becoming a Christian. This was perfect for him!

Mr. McClintock talked of steadfastness and learning to put away the old, sinful things in your life, replacing them with pure, new things. Baptism was a fresh start; one rose out of the watery grave free from their old sins.

After worship service, Parker went to see Mr. McClintock.

"Cliff!" he said, entering the foyer. "What do you think of this?"

Quickly, Parker turned to a page he'd bookmarked in his Bible.

Showing Mr. McClintock, he said, "I found this after the closing prayer. I thought it was a good cross-reference for the priorities people should have."

It was Luke 9:24-26, which said:

*For whosoever will save his life shall lose it: but whosoever will lose his life for my sake, the same shall save it. For what is a man advantaged, if he gain the whole world, and lose himself, or be cast away?*

"That's a great cross-reference, Parker," Mr. McClintock agreed. "It shows the perspective of following Christ. Although the trials may be great—although we may even lose our life—we have a hope of heaven. One may gain everything on earth, but once he dies, it's all gone. Better to store up treasures in heaven, as Matthew 6:19-21 speaks of."

After talking to Cliff, Parker went to find Jacob and Grace. He also talked to many other people on the way to them. There were a lot of new names to memorize, but everyone was incredibly nice.

He couldn't imagine why he ever wanted to stay home on Sundays before. Being with those who wanted to worship God was inspiring. It strengthened him.

And considering the things he was going to be dealing with this week, he needed all the strength he could get.

* * *

Thanksgiving.

While Parker was glad to be with his grandparents for the holiday, it was awkward, since they were atheists like his dad. Being the only Christian around wasn't pleasant.

Mr. Everson was also a bit upset at some more news Parker had given him. Not only had his son become a Christian, but he'd also talked to the elders and officially placed membership at the congregation where the McClintocks attended. Mr. Everson really didn't like that Parker was not only gone on Sundays but also every Wednesday night for Bible study there.

In the past, Thanksgiving had held a different meaning to Parker. He'd been thankful, of course, but he hadn't realized that all the things he felt gratitude for were from God. As he reflected now, he realized how blessed he truly was.

This year, he was especially thankful for something he hadn't previously had: salvation.

After dinner, Parker went to help his grandmother cut the pumpkin pie. He was thinking about how Grace would probably want some, since that was her signature dessert.

Entering the kitchen with some whipped cream, his grandma said, "Parker, I have a question."

"Yes, Grandma?" he asked, feeling his muscles tense. He figured he already knew what she was going to ask.

"Were you... praying before dinner, dear?"

Just as he'd thought. As he always did now, Parker had bowed his head and silently prayed before the meal. He vividly recalled the looks he'd received after, though his family had said nothing.

"Yes, I was," Parker confirmed, putting a slice of pie on a small plate.

"But *why*?" she asked. She didn't seem mad, just very confused.

"Because I'm a Christian now, Grandma," Parker explained.

It was awkward, knowing no one in the house agreed with him. Even so, he had to do the right thing.

"Oh, Parker..." she said with an earnest sigh. "You *know* God's not real."

Following her into the living room with the plates of pie, Parker responded, "But God *is* real. Do you really think you're alive just because of *chance*?"

Mr. Everson gave Parker a look that said something like, "Please behave yourself. Don't act up while we're visiting family on Thanksgiving!"

However, Parker knew the truth needed to be proclaimed.

"Just think about it," he said, keeping his tone low and meek. "What seems more plausible? A divine Creator making the universe, or some random particles floating around and forming atoms? How would we know how those things formed, anyway?"

"Parker," his grandfather began. "You're fifteen. You're too old to believe in fairy tales. Aren't they teaching you about science in school?"

"*Some* of what I'm learning in class is science," Parker replied. "But not the stuff about the Big Bang. No one's observed it, so it can't be science. Evolution isn't science—it's faith. But it's faith without evidence."

"Well, have you *seen* God?"

"Of course not," Parker confirmed. "But I *have* read His word. I have faith in Him because of the Bible and because of the evidence for a Creator. The world is too complex to come about without intelligent design. Believing things came through chance is *blind* faith—that's what belief in the Big Bang is! Evolution says that life came from the nonliving. I can't—"

"Parker," his dad interrupted. "I think that's enough, Son."

Christopher Everson appeared very embarrassed at his boy's words.

Parker's grandmother, wanting to change the subject, said, "So, you feel you're adjusting to Ohio, dear?"

Unfortunately, Parker realized he was going to have to let the previous conversation go.

He nodded. "Yes, Grandma. At first, I really missed the mountains in Wyoming, but I've learned there's something about Ohio's scenery that I like, too. Recently, I've learned change can be good."

Of course, sometimes Parker still longed for the quiet, peaceful nights under the starlit Wyoming heavens. The stars were incredibly bright above his old ranch because there was so little light pollution. Under the blanket of ebony sky, Parker would hear the elk's bugle on summer nights and the coyote's howl.

In winter, he'd hated breaking open the frozen-over water troughs for the animals. But now that those days were gone, sometimes he found himself deeply longing for them. With fondness, he recalled helping his dad with chores on the ranch, regardless of the weather or circumstances. Sometimes that had been hard but taking care of his home had brought him great satisfaction.

It had only been several months since he'd left the beautiful openness of his ranch in Wyoming. Yet, in a way, it felt like much, much longer. He had never expected that his move to the Midwest would be the beginning of his journey to faith.

All these thoughts he kept to himself, deep within his heart, though he longed to share them. His family wouldn't understand his thoughts of faith. They didn't want to.

But he had God's family. The family of the Lord was joined by ties stronger than their own blood. Instead, Christians' ties were held by the blood of Jesus.

What a precious thing it is to be a Christian.

# Trials

## Chapter 11

When Parker got home from school one Wednesday, he headed to his room. Intending to drop off his backpack by the bed and start studying before church, he reached for his Bible in the closet.

As his hand brushed against the shelf, feeling around for God's word, Parker furrowed his brow. Something was out of place. Forehead creased, he slipped his backpack off his shoulder and took a double-look into the wardrobe.

His Bible was gone.

Searching the closet more thoroughly, Parker felt bewildered. It'd been there before he went to school.

What had happened?

Quickly, he looked around his room, and even under his bed. However, his endeavors were fruitless. The Bible was nowhere to be seen.

Embarrassed at losing something so important, Parker walked out of his room and to the dining table, where Mr. Everson was working on bills.

"Dad," he asked, panicked as he ran a hand through his light-brown hair. "Have you seen my Bible?"

Pushing the papers away, Mr. Everson leaned back in his chair. He looked at Parker.

"Son, I think we need to talk."

"Um, okay," Parker replied, quickly sitting down in the wooden chair across from his dad. A twisting feeling was in his stomach.

In the background, the clock ticked routinely, filling the moment of silence. It certainly wasn't ticking as fast as the rhythm in Parker's heart.

"I know you've got good intentions and all," Mr. Everson began. "But this has gone on long enough. I can't have you leaving every Sunday and Wednesday just because you believe—"

"Well, why not?" Parker interrupted. His dad *couldn't* be serious. "I finish all my schoolwork in time, I receive good grades, and I'm not getting into mischief."

"You can't leave for all these church services because the truth is, God's not *real*," Mr. Everson said, almost more like a plea than a statement. "Look, I know you're struggling because Ramona—because your *mother*—left us. It probably makes you feel comforted to believe there's a divine force caring for you. But the thing is, life's just hopeless. We're alone in this world, and when we die, it's all over. That's just *it*."

"No, Dad," Parker said firmly but softly. "While I am hurt horribly over Mom, that's not why I have my faith. I have faith because I have evidence— evidence in the world and in the word. Once we die, that's not just '*it*.' After death, there will be judgment one day. When Christ comes back, I want to go to heaven, and I want you t—"

"Parker," Christopher Everson told him gently. "It's okay to hurt. But we must pick ourselves back up and accept reality."

"That's what I'm *doing*," Parker declared.

"No, you're not," his dad replied, keeping his voice low. "Maybe I should take you to counseling or something. It would probably help—"

"I'm not letting some psychiatrist talk me out of believing in God!" Parker exclaimed, feeling his heart lurch toward his throat. "God's real. Where's my Bible? I've got to study for tonight."

"That's the other thing," Mr. Everson continued. With a sigh, he said, "Look, I'll meet you halfway. You can still go to church on Sundays, but why not just skip out on Wednesdays? You've got school early the next morning anyway."

While perhaps that would sound reasonable to the average listener, Parker couldn't agree. Would the disciples in God's word have made such a deal? No, the men and women in the Bible were persecuted and killed for their willingness to serve the Lord. In the book of Daniel, Daniel was thrown into the lions' den because of praying to God! If they hadn't compromised over their own lives, why would he compromise because of this?

"I can't, Dad," Parker said, rising out of his chair. "I have to obey God."

Specifically, he recalled a verse that Mr. McClintock had given in a recent sermon. As Acts 5:29 said:

*Then Peter and the other apostles answered and said, We ought to obey God rather than men.*

"I'm not saying this because I'm mad at you," Parker said, trying to get Mr. Everson to understand. "I'm doing this because I can't put anything or any*one* above God. Where's my Bible?"

"Inside the safe," Mr. Everson said. "I'm not giving it to you. And I hope you know that's only because I love you and want you to grow up to see reality for all that it is."

Appalled, Parker knew he wasn't going to be able to get his hands on his Bible. He didn't know the safe's passcode. But he still found the hiding place incredibly ironic. Mr. Everson had put God's word in a safe! Since people often put important or treasured possessions in such a place, Parker couldn't hide a smile.

Feeling sure he could borrow a Bible at church, Parker was at least a little comforted. And he could read God's word at home on his computer.

He hated not having his own, physical copy in his hand, with the underlining and notes he'd already begun putting in, but this was the best he could do.

\* \* \*

Mr. Everson was anything but happy that evening. Thankfully, he hadn't further tried to stop his son from going to church, though. After Parker was picked up by the McClintocks, Grace noticed her friend was empty-handed as they got out of the van.

"Where's your Bible?" she whispered. Her blue eyes were incredibly big.

Shaking his head, Parker said, "My dad locked it up in our safe."

"Oh *no*," she breathed, looking deeply concerned. "Nana, Mr. Everson took Parker's Bible away!"

"Did he now?" Mrs. Agnew asked with a tilt of her head. "Well, don't let that stop you. You've got to push beyond what any person on earth thinks of you and focus on how your Father in heaven views you."

By the day, Gwendolyn Agnew seemed to walk a little slower and smile stiffer. The tiredness and pain in her azure eyes could only be concealed so much, and the sight always wrenched Parker's soul.

Often, she still laughed. However, even that was a challenge. Laughing hurt her now, but she just couldn't abstain from it.

Holding the church building's front door opened for the girls, Parker then entered.

"I keep reminding myself of the verses in the Bible about obeying God above anyone else," he told Mrs. Agnew.

"That's right. You keep on obeying and giving it your all," she encouraged. "If you do, you'll be rightly rewarded. God cares for you and treats all with justice. Never forget Matthew 10:37."

Parker could have quoted the verse from memory. He recalled that it ran thus:

*He that loveth father or mother more than me is not worthy of me: and he that loveth son or daughter more than me is not worthy of me.*

Parker thought it was always encouraging to talk to Gwendolyn. Although she struggled so deeply with her health—although her naturally red hair was slowly beginning to fall—she never blamed God. She knew God loved her and that her earthly affliction would only lead to eternal reward. Unless she was too horribly ill, she never missed a worship service.

When Mrs. Agnew was at church, she looked almost healthy. Thoughts of pain were swept away and replaced with thoughts of God's kingdom.

"Keep fighting, Parker," Mrs. Agnew said with a small smile.

"You keep fighting too," Parker whispered to her as he then left to go to his own Bible class. On Wednesdays they were studying the book of Matthew, and Parker really enjoyed it. He soaked up and savored each minute, asking questions, making comments, and learning about Jesus.

He'd gone his whole life not knowing about the One who saved all who would obey. Parker felt he just couldn't get enough of God's word now. He knew the Bible is something you'd never finish studying. There is always a lesson to learn, and learning is hard work.

He also knew how some Christians come to Christ with great zealousness, and then lose their love. He knew that when one makes a commitment to God, they need to remain steadfast all their life.

With the Lord, Parker had meaning in life. He remembered he was made in God's image and was part of His plan. Before his conversion, Parker had felt lost. Everything was empty. Life went on with no greater plan than to try to have a happy enough life and then die. At death, Parker had thought one would just cease to exist, like his dad believed.

But now he knew a soul never dies. For fifteen years, he hadn't realized he'd even had a soul—or that he *was* one—and not just a body.

Though one may be taken and physically harmed or killed for their faith, their persecutors cannot take their soul from them—not unless the oppressed one lets them.

Eternity is a long time. One had better make sure they're spending it in the right place.

* * *

Parker laughed as he sat on the bench, enjoying mint chocolate chip ice cream. It was Friday night, and he'd joined the McClintocks at a local bowling alley.

It was a wonderful Ohio winter night. Snow was falling softly out the windows, making everything feel like a snow globe. Although most of the trees were bare, with their leafless branches pointed toward the sky, evergreens were mixed throughout the landscape.

Even though the sun had long since set (which happened rather early during winters), it was still bright out. There was a full moon, and its beams reflected off the soft, snow, illuminating the night.

Mr. McClintock sure could bowl. Humorously, Parker watched as the man got a spare—knocking down all the remaining pins in the second frame. Then it was Jacob's turn. Following in his father's footsteps, he had the same result. Mrs. McClintock was rather impressive as well.

Meanwhile, Grace was in last place. Although she was not the best bowler by any means, she was entertaining to watch. Other than her, Parker had never seen someone have so much fun getting gutter balls.

Slipping onto the bench at the other side of the table, Grace picked up her strawberry ice cream.

"You did good," she chirped. "I wish I could get even half the pins!"

Parker laughed. During his last efforts, he'd gotten all the pins knocked down but one. Not bad!

"Thanks," he said. "You've just got to find that wrist position I think, Grace. By the way, is the strawberry ice cream good here?"

"Mm-hmm! Look at how fun it is," she said, pushing her container closer to him. "I just love pink sweets."

Smiling, Parker then high fived Jacob as the teen came to join them.

At the sight of her brother, Grace said, "Better watch out, Jacob. Nana's up."

This was one of Mrs. Agnew's good days, which were gradually becoming fewer and farther between. Lately, she'd been struggling to get out of the house as frequently. But this week, she'd felt better, much to everyone's surprise. It had been her idea to get out and have a little fun for the evening. And Gwendolyn

Agnew had always been quite the bowler.

She had to use a lighter ball than in times past, but with ease, she'd just landed a strike!

The company was even better than the bowling—which was saying a lot since everyone, except for Grace, was doing great.

"One day I hope you guys can see my dad bowl," Parker said, wishing Mr. Everson would have joined them. "We used to play a lot, and he's great. Of course, in Wyoming we had to drive a while to get to the nearest bowling alley. But that was okay, because we'd just talk and hang out in our truck. He's also a first-rate gamer. When I was little, I never tired of trying to beat his high scores on our video games."

Parker said this last part with a laugh. He really did love and admire his dad. By no means did the fact that they disagreed change that. But Parker knew he could never let his family overrule his faith.

"Well, I'm off," Parker said, rising to go grab his bowling ball. Then, calling over his shoulder, he added with a laugh, "Jacob, make sure Grace doesn't eat my mint chocolate chip!"

It was nights like these which made Parker reflect on all that he had. Physically, Wyoming was miles away, yet in his heart, parts of it were near. But only parts. A deep place inside him had been reserved for his new life. When he reflected on the gloomy emptiness he'd experienced upon arriving in Ohio, he now thought of the good things he'd obtained.

Things he claimed now were things he'd never have imagined back in Wyoming.

Life is too complex and full for anyone to comprehend. Only God can see what lies ahead. At times, we may feel overwhelmed by change—both good and bad—but God never gives one more than can be handled.

Parker thought of a verse Jacob had mentioned the other day—1 Corinthians 10:13, which read:

*There hath no temptation taken you but such as is common to man: but God is faithful, who will not suffer you to be tempted above that ye are able; but will with the temptation also make a way to escape, that ye may be able to bear it.*

This verse would echo in the back of Parker's mind repeatedly. His family didn't approve of his faith, and sometimes he felt the pressure was too much. After all, he didn't *like* making them disappointed. But no, he knew these were tests for his faith. He could handle them.

With prayer, one can see beyond the trials.

# Comfort in Shadows

## Chapter 12

U sually, Mr. Everson drove Parker to school in the mornings. Occasionally, however, he couldn't because he was called out to work earlier.

Parker disliked riding the bus. Jeb and Ivan whispered and laughed about him, plenty loud enough for Parker to hear, and someone was always complaining it seemed. More so, it wasn't uncommon to find an old, moldy cheese stick or a random sock lying on the floor. Obviously, students could be a little... weird. Yes, it was just an all-around unpleasant experience, even if the bus driver was nice and courteous.

In the past, Parker would pull out his Bible and quietly read it, but now he couldn't do that. Instead, he read over his homework.

When he arrived at school, he thanked the bus driver, waved, and then sighed, glad to get out of the small, crowded space. Soon, he spotted Grace, who was as cheerful as ever, and they made their way to biology class.

"Bowling was so much fun, wasn't it?" she piped up as she slipped into her seat.

"Mm-hmm," Parker agreed. "Great job on getting that spare at the end."

"It was about time!" Grace chirped with a merry giggle. "Maybe I'm starting to warm up. I nearly screamed when the final pen tipped over. Hey Parker, when are we going to dissect frogs? I'm *really* not looking forward to that."

Laughing a bit at her quick conversation change, Parker replied, "I'm not sure, but probably toward the end of the school year."

"Well, I wish we didn't have to do it at *all*," Grace replied, blue eyes wide and serious. "I just love frogs—they're my favorite animal, tied with Tabitha."

As he recalled the cuddly feline, Parker nodded in understanding. Everyone loved Tabitha.

The lesson soon started, though with no dissecting, thankfully. They were learning about the basic structures of plants. Grace was much more enthusiastic about this and kept on raising her hand to answer questions.

It was during Mr. Granger's side-point lecture on photosynthesis that the door opened a crack.

Turning his head to the entrance, the teacher asked, "Jacob, aren't you supposed to be in your own class?"

After all, he was a junior, not a freshman.

"I have permission," Jacob said, now stepping into the room. "I'm supposed to get Grace."

The girl's eyes went very wide and there was a deep, anxious look in them. Like the busting of glass, the previous cheerfulness Grace had shown that morning was now gone. She seemed to know something, but Parker didn't understand what.

Biting his lip, Jacob then said, "It's Nana. Come on, we've got to go, Sis."

Quickly, Grace turned to Mr. Granger, who nodded in permission, and she rose to her feet. In an instant, the two siblings were gone.

Parker felt his heart speed up. What was wrong?

* * *

Although Mr. Everson had to leave earlier than usual for work that day, he was rewarded with getting home sooner. Therefore, he was at the house when Parker arrived, and had gotten a phone call about the

McClintocks.

So, as soon as Parker was back from school, the teen learned what was wrong. Gwendolyn Agnew was in the hospital, and she was very, very sick.

"Dad," he said, "she's my friends' nana. I want to go see her—can we?"

He was worried, and Christopher Everson could tell. His somewhat reserved son rarely showed so much concern.

Knowing this was clearly important to Parker, Mr. Everson nodded.

"I'll call and check if it's okay for visitors, and if so, we'll go."

While his dad went to make the phone call, Parker went to his room and shut the door. He needed some quiet time to pray fervently for Mrs. Agnew and for the McClintocks. When he finished, Parker took a deep breath and left his room. Praying gave him strength, because he was confident the Lord heard him.

Although Parker didn't know what God's answer would be, he knew He would answer. Everything was in God's hands.

When the Eversons got confirmation that it was all right to go, they left at once.

"Thanks for taking me, Dad," Parker said, voice sounding hollow.

It was a dreary, gray day. The clouds were vast, enveloping the sky and concealing the sun. Matching the heavens was the ground, covered in a thick blanket of snow. On top of everything, the wind blew bitterly, and the temperature was in the single digits.

At least the roads were cleared of snow properly.

Parker stared out of the passenger seat's window, feeling that joy was far from him. On this part of the road, the evergreens were few and far between, so most of the trees were just spindly, bare things. They looked as empty as Parker's heart was beginning to feel. Light seemed to fade. When Jacob came to class to fetch Grace, Parker had detected the clear urgency in the brother's tone.

To Parker, it seemed the cloudy skies would cover the world for a very long time.

Eventually, they arrived at the hospital. It was a big building with twelve floors and an innumerable number of staff. At least Gwendolyn had got help immediately, thanks to the many workers.

Absentmindedly, Parker followed his dad inside and waited as Mr. Everson talked to a woman at the front desk. They were given instructions on how to get to Mrs. Agnew's room, and then walked up five flights of stairs. Although it was a shame that the elevators had just gone out-of-order, neither Everson had ever liked elevators anyway. To Parker, they were small and cramped, and malfunctioned far too often. It was a phobia, one might say.

Gently knocking on the room's door, Mr. Everson looked at his son and gave him a small pat on the shoulder. Parker's father had never met the McClintocks, and meeting at a hospital was a rather undesirable place.

Jacob answered the door and invited them inside. Quietly, Parker introduced his dad and then was nearly crushed in a hug by Grace. She looked very vulnerable.

After the hug was released and Parker could breathe again, he took in the sight of Gwendolyn Agnew, feeling shattered.

Cliff and Katie McClintock were sitting on a couple of chairs on the right side of the bed. Evidently, Cliff had been reading the Bible to his mother-in-law before the Eversons came in. Katie's eyes were red and her cheeks tearstained.

Parker had never seen her like this. She looked so abundantly helpless.

Gwendolyn breathed in deeply, yet slowly. The hospital bed seemed massive compared to the frail woman inside it. Yet, her blue eyes met Parker's gray ones, holding their usual bright curiosity.

"… Parker Everson… who've you brought with you today?"

"This is my dad," Parker introduced to Mrs. Agnew. "Christopher Everson."

She gave a smile that, though tight and filled with pain, was as sincere as ever.

"I'm happy to finally meet you, Mr. Everson. Parker talks of you often. Unfortunately, you seem to have caught me at a bad time."

"I'm very sorry you're sick," Mr. Everson replied. "Is there anything I can get you?"

"Oh no," Mrs. Agnew answered with the same smile she'd shown a moment ago. Nodding her head toward the Bible in Cliff's hands, she said, "I've got all I need right here."

With a shakiness in her voice, she continued. "There's my own Bible on the counter over there. But I'm so tired, I feel like I need my family to read to me. Now that Parker's here, though, I think I've got an idea. Jacob, would you grab my Bible for me?"

Jacob quickly did so, handing it to his nana. The Bible's cover was very dark green, nearly black, and it was lined in decorative strips of gold.

"Oh, yes, thank you dear," she replied, taking a labored breath and repositioning herself deeper into her bed. "Come over here, Parker."

Confused, he walked over and sat on the edge of the bed as she prompted him.

"There we go," she said contently, leaning back and closing her eyes briefly. "Here Parker, I want you to have this. Now, Mr. Everson, don't go taking it away from him, he needs this to get him through life and to eternity. I wish you'd read it too. Go on, take it Parker. It's yours now."

She pressed the dark-evergreen-colored Bible in his hands with her own ice-cold ones, and then gave

Mr. Everson a look that suggested he ought to take her words to heart.

"Oh no, I can't accept this," Parker said quickly. "This is yours. You're going to need it when we get you back to church, Gwen."

"I'm going to paradise, Parker," Gwendolyn said with soft laugh and a radiant smile. For a moment, the pain was gone in her face. "I can't take this leatherbound Bible with me. So, you just keep it with you and read it cover to cover."

Parker felt a lump rising in his throat and tears threatening to spring up in eyes. Anxiously, he said, "But you're going to get better. You're—"

"Parker, why don't you read to me?" Gwendolyn Agnew asked. "I want to hear what Paul told Timothy in 2 Timothy 4:6-8."

With trembling hands, he turned to the requested passage. In a quivering voice, the teenager read aloud:

*"For I am now ready to be offered, and the time of my departure is at hand. I have fought a good fight, I have finished my course, I have kept the faith: Henceforth there is laid up for me a crown of righteousness, which the Lord, the righteous judge, shall give me at that day: and not to me only, but unto all them also that love his appearing."*

In a quiet voice, Gwendolyn Agnew said, "Just

think, everyone. I'm going to be with the writer of that passage soon."

* * *

Ecclesiastes 7 rightly says: *A good name is better than precious ointment; and the day of death than the day of one's birth. It is better to go to the house of mourning, than to go to the house of feasting: for that is the end of all men; and the living will lay it to his heart. Sorrow is better than laughter: for by the sadness of the countenance the heart is made better. The heart of the wise is in the house of mourning; but the heart of fools is in the house of mirth.*

Gwendolyn Agnew died only an hour after Parker read in 2 Timothy for her about fighting a good fight and obtaining a crown of righteousness. Unlike others, she passed away with a smile on her lips. He knew the name "Gwendolyn" would always hold a special meaning for him, for she'd shown him what it meant to serve God through terrible storms. She'd encouraged Parker's spirit greatly over the months he'd known her. No matter what, he was confident that he had to fight a good fight like she did. He was determined to win.

Now, two days had passed since her death, and Parker went with his dad to the McClintocks' to comfort them. The house Parker had always loved to visit for its warmth and joy was truly a house of mourning today. There was a strange, empty feeling within.

Grace opened the door for him, and her blue eyes were glassy and red. She sounded stuffed up from crying.

"Oh, Grace," Parker murmured, giving her a warm, long hug. "I'm so sorry."

Her breaths were shaky, and she wiped her tears away with a loud sniff.

"Thank you for coming," she replied softly. "I'm so happy that Nana isn't hurting anymore, but... but *I* still hurt so much."

"I know," Parker replied. He tried to think of something more to say, but his mind second-guessed every phrase that entered his head. However, Grace just seemed to want someone nearby. Perhaps she didn't need words of comfort any more than a familiar, loving presence.

At this moment, Tabitha bounded down the stairs and let out a raspy meow.

"Oh, *Tabitha*," Grace breathed, reaching down and gathering the soft feline into her arms. Turning to Parker, she then said, "She's my cat now... Nana said she wanted me to take care of her."

Gently, she stroked Tabitha's soft fur coat, and sat down on the couch, patting an empty seat to suggest that Parker join her.

"Isn't she sweet?" Grace asked with a sniff, tilting her head to Tabitha. "I think she really misses Nana. She just doesn't understand."

The loyal cat burrowed down in Grace's arms

and let out a soft meow. She did certainly seem confused.

"It is a great comfort to me," Grace began, "to think that Nana's not really *gone*. She still exists. She's only traveled on."

"Now she doesn't hurt anymore," Parker agreed mildly. "Jacob and I talked about how the angels carry the righteous off to paradise when they die, like Luke 16:22 says. It's an amazing thought, thinking of them bringing all of God's saints onward."

Grace smiled, her glassy blue eyes reflecting the fireplace light.

"It is a beautiful concept," she concurred, tilting her head as she thought deeply. "And soon, Christ will come back, and the dead will be raised. Then all of God's children will go to heaven."

Comfort in Christ is a comfort like none other.

# Part 4

*I fit in this eternal plan!*

*I'm held within God's holy hand*

*Your faith I call reality*

*Devout joy strengthens me.*

# Truth's Echo

## Chapter 13

The cold darkness following Gwendolyn Agnew's death settled over her loved ones for days. But life is full of seasons, and none remain forever. In time, the snow and ice gradually melted, sinking into the earth, and the sun chased the clouds away. Bare branches from trees and bushes budded, then bursting forth into leaves and flowers.

While everyone still missed Mrs. Agnew, they found relief from the dull aches in their hearts. Her death motivated everyone to serve God more diligently. If one obeys and is faithful until death, they have their reward, and they'll be with all the saints forevermore.

One clear April day, Parker bought a large bouquet of forget-me-nots and went to the cemetery. He hadn't visited Gwen's grave in a while, and he had a longing to visit.

Walking across the soft grass, Parker acknowledged the sweet notes of singing birds and the slight chill that still lingered in the breeze. In time, winter's last breaths would completely die away.

Cemeteries are a quiet place to reflect on the past and ponder the future. Very clearly, Parker still remembered the dreary, dark-clouded day when he'd attended Mrs. Agnew's graveside service. Yet, even amid the storm, there was hope. His dad had come with him to the service, which he'd been very grateful for.

As Parker placed the forget-me-nots on Mrs. Agnew's grave, he bowed his head and prayed to the Lord, finding great solace.

Lately, he found himself thinking much more of heaven. He didn't know what day the dead would rise and join their Savior above, but it was a beautiful thought. He wanted to be ready for that event.

If only more people would prepare for Judgment Day!

This sin-tainted world can only bring so much joy. It is a sad thought that for many; the earth is the best they will ever have. But anyone can turn from their sins and follow Jesus if they choose to obey Him diligently.

Finishing his prayer, Parker knelt by the grave. A soft ray of sunlight warmed his face, drying the tears that slipped down his cheeks. Gwendolyn's headstone was engraved for both her and her husband. Parker stared at the first line of text on her side of the tombstone:

MRS. GWENDOLYN ELISE AGNEW

"I have Nana's middle name."

Nearly jumping from surprise, Parker turned around and saw Grace. In the distance, the rest of the McClintocks were walking toward them in the cemetery. He'd had no idea that they would all be there that day.

Rising, Parker replied, "Your name's Grace Elise?"

"Mm-hmm," Grace confirmed, looking down at the headstone. "Since it's a family name, Mom has it too. It means 'God is my oath.' What's your middle name?"

"Joshua," Parker said. "When they picked it, I don't think my parents were considering the man in the Bible, though."

Tilting her head and curving her lips into a smile, Grace said, "I think that means 'Jehovah is salvation.'"

"Really?" Parker asked, suddenly feeling as bright as the sun's rays. "Although my parents didn't have the meaning in mind, I'm glad they gave it to me."

Grace nodded. "My family and I didn't expect to see anyone else here. Mom's brought some roses for the grave."

The rest of the McClintocks were caught up to them now.

"I see," Parker replied. "Yeah, I wanted to bring some flowers, too. Gwen deserves an entire garden of them, you know."

Letting out a soft sigh, Grace agreed, "I think so too. Thank you for bringing some, that's really nice. Is it just you here today?"

"Mm-hmm. Dad's going to pick me up later, but he went to run some errands. Cemeteries are interesting places, wouldn't you say?" Parker asked as he started to walk away, looking at some of the other tombstones.

It was an old cemetery, raised on a slight hill and with many buried there for a couple of hundred years. Perhaps some people only found such places frightening, but Parker saw them as sobering.

"Yes, graveyards are very interesting," Grace concurred, following him. "In cemeteries, it's like time just stops. Over there, past the fence, the cars wiz by and everyone's busy going from place to place. Right now, those people aren't really *thinking*, just existing. Here, it's different, at least for me. See those dates on the stones?"

"Yeah?"

"They're more than just numbers," Grace said decidedly. "They're lives. I wonder what these peoples' days were like. I don't want to live a life full of regrets. You've only got so much time between the moment you're born and the moment you die."

As depressing as it may have sounded, Grace's words were true. But if one is living for God, is death truly so dreary? According to Ecclesiastes, it isn't.

Parker talked with her for a while, until he saw his dad's pickup, and he knew he'd better get going. Besides, Grace probably wanted to spend some time with her family at the grave. Briefly, he talked with the rest of the McClintocks before he left.

"That was nice of you to bring those flowers," his dad said as Parker jumped into the passenger seat of the big, black truck.

Nodding absentmindedly, Parker stared out of the window toward the cemetery until they turned onto a different road, and it vanished from sight.

"I think the McClintocks will be all right," he said, almost to himself. "God and the brethren have been helping them through."

Mr. Everson did not say anything. Thankfully, he hadn't taken the Bible Gwendolyn had given Parker away. And he no longer tried to keep him from church.

"There weren't many people at the cemetery," Parker said, turning to his dad. "But the McClintocks came just after me. It was really sobering in there."

"Those places tend to be that way," Mr. Everson replied, concentrating on the road.

"Dad," Parker said slowly, "are you afraid to die?"

"I suppose everyone is," he responded, not exactly answering him straightly.

"Maybe not everyone," Parker said. "Of course, it seems a little scary since no one knows what it's like to be a soul separated from their body…"

At the stoplight, Mr. Everson was again silent, but gave Parker a look—one the teen just couldn't place.

* * *

"Today, class, we're going to be working on an essay that will make up a quarter of your grade for this unit," Mr. Granger said, walking down the rows and passing out papers. "Everyone have one? Good. I think this will be good practice, because you'll have to put all your knowledge down in a limited amount of time. We'll begin now!"

Gazing down at the sheet on his desk, Parker felt his heart flutter. This biology unit had been a *very* unpleasant one.

The essay's prompt was about explaining the concept of natural selection, and why it is known as scientific "fact." Parker thought it was ridiculous.

One would have to ignore things about how to prove that something is scientific fact to say that natural selection was.

Twisting around in her seat, Grace shot Parker a glance that revealed she shared his displeasure.

In the past, Parker would have just gone along with the prompt. But he remembered the day that Grace had triumphantly received an F. She didn't let anything make her renounce God's word. Now, he wasn't going to either.

Grabbing his pencil, Parker inhaled deeply but quietly, and then began to write. A wave of nervousness washed over him, and he bounced his foot vigorously until a boy on his left whispered, asking him to stop.

Dutifully, Parker wrote:

> *Natural selection is believed to be how species' bodies adapt to their environment. In our textbooks, it is mentioned that penguins cannot fly. Apparently, this is supposed to confirm the view. It is claimed that the penguins adapted to their location by losing their capability to take flight.*
>
> *However, we see no evidence for this, and even if a flying penguin could be observed, it'd still just be a penguin. No new genetic information exists. Instead, penguins have lost genetic information!*

*We also hear of, for example, vestigial organs. It is believed that these organs were once useful but are now apparently useless. Some claim that tonsils are an example of such, because they can be removed from someone, and they were once thought to not hold any purpose. It is claimed that this is an example of an organ that was once useful to humans but has become useless.*

*Is this true, though? No! On the contrary, tonsils, when healthy, are useful parts of the immune system. Instead of them proving natural selection, they are evidence of an all-wise Creator who gives us an abundance for our wellbeing! Finally, it is also believed that natural selection can give rise to new species from an old one. But where have we ever seen anything supporting this? Are not penguins still birds? Truly, our Creator made everything after its own kind, as shown in Genesis 1:24-25. There may be different breeds—or variations—in a kind, but they are all still the same kind.*

Scanning over his work a couple of times, Parker leaned back in relief. It felt good to write what was in his heart, even if he knew his teacher was going to disagree. Just because people agree with someone, that doesn't mean they've done the right thing.

It doesn't matter what anyone says. All that matters is that God is pleased.

Mr. Granger cleared his throat, then saying, "I think everyone's about done with their drafts. How about we have some of you guys that are feeling confident come up and read your work?"

Before he knew what he was doing, Parker shot his hand up.

"Parker," the teacher said, calling on him. "All right, how about you show us what you've got."

Grabbing his paper, Parker Everson walked to the front of the class. He knew Mr. Granger would probably never call on him to read again after this. But truth needed to echo through this school's walls. He wanted his classmates to hear an alternative view to the things everyone had been studying.

The sea of faces peered at him, some interested, others bored-to-death. For a moment, Parker froze and couldn't find his voice. It was not often he spoke in front of the class.

He saw Grace smiling at him from the crowd. She appeared eager, attentive, and trusting. She was relying on him to reveal the truth and expose the error to everyone in this room. He wasn't going to let her down. And most importantly, he wasn't going to let God down.

Clearing his throat, Parker read determinedly.

"Natural selection is believed to be how species'

bodies adapt to their environment. In our textbooks, it is mentioned that penguins cannot fly. Apparently, this is supposed to confirm the view…"

In a moment, he was sure more than one face would be scowling.

"… It is claimed that the penguins adapted to their location by losing their capability to take flight," Parker said, lifting his eyes and establishing eye contact. "However, we see no evidence for this, and even if a flying penguin could be observed, it'd still just be a penguin. No new genetic information exists. Instead, penguins have lost genetic information!"

He could feel the eyes staring at him—some in surprised curiosity, others in annoyance. And with one pair of bright blue eyes, he could feel pure admiration.

Parker continued with the essay bravely, and then coming toward the end, felt a wave of determination and thanksgiving. He was so grateful to God for creating the world. He was so grateful to Him for His intelligent design. God always knew best.

Speaking loud and clear, Parker concluded his essay. "Truly, our Creator made everything after its own kind, as shown in Genesis 1:24-25. There may be different breeds—or variations—in a kind, but they are all still the same kind."

There was a long moment of silence. Everyone was staring. Some were clearly gazing in a way that revealed they'd been daydreaming and not listening at all. But others had heard every word. Clearly, Grace wanted to applaud. But instead, she smiled in her radiant way which always made Parker wonder how her face didn't hurt long afterward.

The heavy silence caused Parker's heart to thump vigorously from nervousness. By now, he began to wonder if everyone could hear it.

"Um... thank you, Mr. Everson," Mr. Granger said, taken aback by his student's essay. "You may sit down."

Slipping into his seat, Parker didn't care one bit about the rotten score he was surely going to receive. When he considered everything his Creator had given him, one bad grade was hardly something to complain about.

# An Essay's Performance

## Chapter 14

The next week, Parker received back his essay, grade and all. Obviously, it was not a score the average student would be happy about. Although disappointed that he had to receive such a grade in the first place, he felt better about doing the right thing than having a good score.

To Parker's surprise, he hadn't actually received an F. Rather, he'd been given a D and some feedback.

In red ink, Mr. Granger had written,

> *While your essay is the complete opposite of what you were instructed to write, I'm impressed that you spoke your mind so boldly. I don't agree with your perspective, but I'm not giving you a failing grade. Stick to the prompt next time.*

Although a D certainly was not a good grade, it *was* better than an F. And Parker wasn't alone because Grace had stood up for her beliefs too. It's always nice to have someone else to relate with but he knew he'd need to do the right thing, Grace or no Grace. And as for Mr. Granger's request about next time, Parker knew he'd have to write whatever the truth was, regardless of the circumstances.

Among his family, Parker was a loner. He didn't expect his dad or relatives to appreciate the things he would do. They didn't understand why he prayed. And even if his family *had* believed in God, he figured they might still think it wise to write the essay the way the teacher had wanted it written—and not the way it had *needed* to be written.

Unfortunately, it seemed that his family viewed him as the relative who pretended to live in a fantasy world. If Parker truly believed God was a fairy tale though, he wouldn't have forfeited his grade. By then, it would have been time to wake up.

There is a moment in everyone's life where they stop believing in the make-believe. But the Bible is no work of fiction. God is the reason for our existence and the meaning in our lives.

"Parker? I'm home!"

Wiping his floured hands on his black apron, Parker then waved as his dad walked in. The teenager was making his best attempt at baking a chicken pot pie.

"Hey, Dad, how was work?"

"Good enough," Mr. Everson answered. "What've you got here? Chicken pot pie, hmm? Sounds good to me! Here, let me help you."

He started rolling out the pie crust, letting Parker work on cutting the chicken, and then asked how school was.

"Pretty good, except I got a bad grade," Parker explained, feeling his stomach flip-flop in nervousness. He wondered what his dad was going to say when he found out the cause of his great, big, red D.

"Oh? Well, what class?"

"Biology. I nearly failed my essay," Parker explained, finishing the chicken.

"You *failed*?" Mr. Everson asked, looking up from his perfectly formed pie shell and widening his gray eyes. "What happened?"

"I *almost* failed. I think I'll just show you the paper," Parker replied, rinsing his hands and then heading for his room. A moment later, he'd retrieved it from the blue folder in his backpack and placed it on the kitchen counter.

Grabbing it, Mr. Everson read in silence. While he waited for his dad's response, Parker filled the pie shell with the chicken, and stirred the gravy. In a moment, Mr. Everson grabbed a magnet and placed the essay with its enormous, bright-red D on the fridge door—a rather unusual display. Then, still without speaking, Mr. Everson started working on the top crust.

"Well?" Parker questioned as the gravy started to simmer. "Aren't you going to say something?"

"I'm thinking," Mr. Everson replied, staring down at the rolled-out dough.

As the gravy finished, Parker poured it over the chicken in the pie shell. Watching his dad crimping the top crust around the edges of the pan, Parker sighed softly. Vividly, he recalled the many times, years ago, that he'd seen his dad help his mom make chicken pot pies. Parker was relieved that, as they worked, Mr. Everson didn't appear depressed from those bittersweet memories. Parker had been hoping his dad wouldn't mind the familiar meal.

At last, Mr. Everson said softly, "You've never been one for troublemaking before."

Sucking in his breath, Parker widened his eyes. "It's not that at all, Dad! I just *couldn't* follow the assignment—not when it's wrong."

Being thought of as a troublemaker was even worse than being thought of as a delusional fantasy believer.

Mr. Everson cut a few slits as vents in the center of the pie crust, and then put the chicken pot pie in the oven. Before going to wash a bowl, he looked Parker straight in his gray eyes, which were so like his own.

"I don't suppose *you* of all people would be likely to get a bad grade for stirring up something," Mr. Everson said, reaching for the dish soap. "And knowing you, I'm sure you could have got a higher grade if you wanted to."

It was true. Parker had understood exactly what his teacher had wanted him to write, and also knew just how to craft the manuscript. He could have probably got an A easily enough. But instead, he'd turned his essay into a paper refuting what the class had been taught.

"They needed to hear the truth, Dad," Parker responded earnestly. "Who's going to encourage them to think for themselves? When I was converted, I weighed up both sides. But it wasn't easy. At first, I wanted to believe what I'd been told my whole life!"

"And what changed your mind?" Mr. Everson asked. This felt like the first time since Parker's conversion that his dad asked about his faith and wanted to genuinely know the answer.

"So *many* things," Parker declared. "I saw the trees, the sky, the birds... They're so complex, Dad—too complex to exist from chance. And yet, they don't even compare to *people*. There's so much evidence for an intelligent, divine Creator. And when I compared the reasons for my beliefs of evolution, I realized how it just didn't make sense! An entire universe of living things coming from some non-living particles? I don't think so. But that's not all."

Parker took a deep breath, before continuing. "I read the Bible. Dad, it's God's inspired word, penned by different men over years and years. Yet even though so many people wrote it through the generations, it never contradicts itself. If those men weren't inspired by the Holy Spirit, surely there would be a lot of mistakes. The Bible told me how the world came to be, and the plan God formed for man—the plan of redemption."

Pulling up a chair and sitting down, Mr. Everson replied, "I see. And how do you explain all the bad things in the world? Why did Ramona leave us? And why did your God let your friends' grandmother die?"

"Because God doesn't wrap His creations up in bubble wrap," Parker said honestly. Taking a chair for himself, he sat on it backward, resting his arms on the top of the chair's back. "Mom left us because God gives everyone free will. Sometimes having free will means people get hurt and hurt others. What

Mom did is wrong—sinful. And as for Gwen's passing… When sin entered the world, so did disease and death. It's not a pain-free world, it's a *free will* world. If life was perfect, would anyone really aspire to go to heaven? Just think, Dad. Although Gwen's dead, she's not suffering anymore. Because she served God until death, she's in paradise right now."

Parker paused, collecting his thoughts. Then, feeling strengthened for everything he believed in, he continued, "That's why people live for Christ and die for Him—because He's good and faithful and rewards everyone who serves Him. Earth isn't where life ends, it's just where our test begins. If we pass the test, we'll be with God forever. And if we fail…" he trailed, looking earnestly at his dad. Parker hated thinking about Mr. Everson's own current standing with God, considering it wasn't a good one. "If we fail, we don't have that reward. Maybe that's why some people choose to try to reject God's existence. They want to believe this earth is all there is, because then they can deny that hell exists. But heaven and hell are both equally real."

Thinking over Parker's long speech, Mr. Everson said nothing. The only noise in the room was the rigid ticking of the clock on the wall. Noiselessly, Parker got up from his chair and went to his room.

Grabbing his Bible, which was once Gwendolyn Agnew's, Parker held it close to his chest, feeling his heart thump in rhythm with the clock. He missed the kind and zealous elderly lady that had encouraged him in his walk with Christ.

"Here, Dad," he said, navigating through the worn-out pages. Turning to Hebrews 9:27-28, he read aloud:

*"And as it is appointed unto men once to die, but after this the judgment: So Christ was once offered to bear the sins of many; and unto them that look for him shall he appear the second time without sin unto salvation."*

Again, he was met with silence. Mr. Everson leaned over and looked at the verses for himself. Then he asked, "The death is the crucifixion, right?"

"Yes," Parker agreed, nodding, pleased that his dad was asking him questions about the Bible. "Because of their sins, humanity is utterly lost. But Jesus has died for everyone, and has provided a sacrifice for the world, because He, the Son of God, never once sinned. With Christ's blood, we can be redeemed from our sins. But only if we believe Him and obey Him faithfully all our lives. See what it says here in Acts 2:38? After Jesus's crucifixion, look what these people were told to do: *Then Peter said unto them, Repent, and be baptized every one of you in the name of Jesus Christ for the remission of sins, and ye shall receive the gift of the Holy Ghost."*

"If all of this is true," Mr. Everson started slowly,

"then you're saying I'm lost."

"Well... what is the Bible saying, Dad?"

Mr. Everson did not reply, but Parker knew his father understood the answer.

"Look, Dad," Parker said, getting up and turning off the oven, then pulling the chicken pot pie out. "When someone isn't right with God, they're lost—whether they believe in His existence or not. But anyone can be saved if they are only willing to believe, repent of their sins, confess Jesus, and then be buried with Him in baptism."

Parker sat back down by his dad and turned to various passages as confirmation. He found the ones that he remembered Mr. McClintock showing him before his own conversion and also some other ones that he'd heard in the sermons recently and had written in his notebook.

Parker talked a long while, and Mr. Everson mostly said nothing, though occasionally he asked a question or made an argument. As time went on, however, Mr. Everson seemed to run out of things to say.

The chicken pot pie was long forgotten, cooling on the counter. The more Parker spoke, the more verses he recalled. Amazed, he was pleased to notice he could remember where the different references were located and turn to them quickly. With study, he'd really been memorizing a lot more than he'd realized.

It was a fantastic feeling, seeing different parts of the Bible coming together, like a perfectly fitting puzzle. Parker was one of those pieces in God's plan; he was the redeemed.

"Look at what the apostle Paul was told before his own conversion, back when he was named Saul," Parker said, turning to Acts. "Dad, these words apply to us today, because we live in the New Testament. Acts 22:16 reads, *And now why tarriest thou? arise, and be baptized, and wash away thy sins, calling on the name of the Lord.* Why are *you* delaying, Dad? Is it because you still don't believe? Or is it because you're like I was—afraid? What is it?"

"I'm forty-four," Mr. Everson replied dryly. "I've lived this way my whole life, and now I'm hearing I'm supposed to change."

"So, you *are* afraid then," Parker answered in understanding. "Dad, you're afraid of living differently. But you tell me: Is it better to live the rest of your life the same way you always have, because it's what you're used to and comfortable with? Or is it better to change now and remain faithful, so that you're secure with God for all of eternity? You tell me."

The clock's ticking seemed to echo in Parker's ears, and then Mr. Everson said, "You've got me there. Four decades doesn't look very long compared to forever."

"So do you believe in God?" Parker asked, then

holding his breath.

"Your steadfastness has blown me away," Mr. Everson said with a small laugh. "I guess I've been thinking about this stuff for a little while now—ever since Mrs. Agnew died. Really, Parker, I can see that you have full belief and confidence in the things and passages you've told me. And that essay of yours, though deemed a D by your teacher, gets an A in my eyes. Yes, I believe God exists."

Parker felt like his heart was going to explode.

"Well, are you going to obey Him? Or are you going to make yourself miserable and try to resist like I did?"

"Put that pot pie in the fridge," Mr. Everson said, standing up. "I'm done with living the way I have. I'm going to obey our Creator."

Parker jumped from his seat. In an instant, he was stashing the dinner away and grabbing the telephone. Dialing, he then heard Cliff McClintock pick up.

"Hello?"

"Hello, Cliff! This is Parker Everson."

Over the phone, Mr. McClintock replied, "Hey Parker! You sound happy. What's going on?"

Taking a deep breath, he couldn't hold back his grin.

"My dad wants to become a Christian."

# Hope

## Chapter 15

There was a great sweetness in Parker's heart—an everlasting treasury in his memory. As he and his dad rode in their truck toward the church building, he nearly felt like he could sing with gladness—and he was not one to often sing.

His dad was going to be saved! Now Parker would no longer be alone in his family. He'd never thought a move to Ohio could change his world in such a way.

It is a precious, wonderful thing to believe God and obey Him. When we put our full trust in our Lord, we have peace like none other, and a joy that cannot be extinguished. Life's cares and troubles do not seem so great or burdensome with the Father, Son, and Holy Spirit.

The McClintocks were also on their way to the church building. Since they lived a little closer, they'd already gone inside and turned on all the lights and such by the time Parker and his dad arrived.

"When you're baptized, hold your nose, Dad," Parker said, recalling what Grace had once told him. He got out of the truck and walked across the parking lot to the church building. "That way the water won't go up."

Mr. Everson grinned at Parker. As they walked up the steps, Parker looked toward the large stone welcome sign which was at the left side of the building. In clean, bold print it read:

CHURCH OF CHRIST ASSEMBLES HERE.

Entering the church building, Parker could not hold back a grin. As largely as he was smiling, he was almost beginning to look like Grace.

"Parker!"

Speaking of Grace, she appeared in the foyer and gave him a happy hug. In an instant, Jacob also came over, and clapped Parker on the back.

"Hey man, this is great news," he cheered. "I'm so glad your dad and you are going to strive for the same goal now—heaven."

"Me too," Parker said, his heart feeling incredibly light as Mr. McClintock talked to Mr. Everson, explaining some things.

Following his friends to the front pew, Parker then sat down. He waved to Katie McClintock, who beamed at him, and then talked quietly with her in excitement.

With fondness, Parker recalled his own conversion. Back then, he'd been getting ready in one of the small rooms, but now he sat on the pews with the others. This time, he was going to watch someone else obey the Lord, and that someone was his own dad!

Remembering Mrs. Agnew sitting on one of the pews and smiling at him—looking so healthy from her joy—Parker felt his heart ache. Even though she wasn't suffering anymore, a part of him still wished she could be with them this day. How exuberant she would be, seeing that now Parker's dad also believed!

While Mr. Everson was getting ready, Jacob got up and started leading a hymn. As Parker sung, he couldn't stop smiling. Afterward, Jacob then asked him if he'd like to lead a hymn also.

In the past, the thought of leading singing had terrified Parker. But now, his dad was becoming a Christian. Surely now of all times Parker could step out of his comfort zone!

"I'll lead one," Parker said determinedly,

standing up as Katie and Grace smiled at him encouragingly. He went to the podium and turned through the hymnal to find the song he wanted.

Finding it, he smiled. He'd turned to one of the same hymns he remembered being led at his own conversion. It was a joyous song of the faith and trust of following Jesus.

With strength in his voice and gladness in his heart, he led the hymn. Only he and the McClintocks were here, so it was less intimidating for him. If he'd been leading in front of everyone at church, the sea of faces would make him nervous. But even so, he realized now that he wanted to push himself further out of his comfort zone—he wanted to lead in worship service in any way that he could. Maybe not right away, but gradually, he wanted to do more for this congregation.

It seemed perfect timing that when he finished the hymn, Mr. McClintock and Mr. Everson were now ready.

Quietly, Parker went to sit down between Jacob and Grace.

Mr. McClintock looked Mr. Everson straight in the eyes and said, "Do you believe Jesus is the Son of God and that He died for your sins?"

Nodding, Mr. Everson said, "Yes, I do."

"I now baptize you in the name of the Father, the Son, and the Holy Spirit."

Quickly, Mr. McClintock dunked him down into

the watery grave and lifted him up.

"2 Corinthians 5:17 says, *Therefore if any man be in Christ, he is a new creature: old things are passed away; behold, all things are become new.* Congratulations, Brother!" Mr. McClintock said. "Your sins are washed away. Now you're part of God's family."

Mr. Everson smiled so largely that in any other circumstance, it would have caught Parker by surprise. How wonderful it is to do God's will!

There were a couple more hymns, with Parker leading the last one. Then the door to one of the small rooms opened and Mr. Everson came out, hair wet from the baptism. Setting the hymnal down, Parker left the podium and gave his dad a tight hug.

"Dad!" he breathed. "I'm so proud of you. You did the right thing."

Everyone was talking and congratulating Mr. Everson.

Coming out of one of the other small rooms, Mr. McClintock congratulated Mr. Everson. Then, turning to Parker, Cliff said, "I'm sure happy for you. With both you and your dad fighting the good fight, I know you're both going to be strengthened. And you did great leading singing for the first time!"

For a long time, everyone lingered, talking. Then, to Parker's delight, his dad invited the McClintocks over. After all, the Eversons hadn't had their pot pie dinner. Why not enjoy it with friends?

Before they left the church building, they had a prayer. As Parker exited, he felt that the fresh spring world of April was incredibly bright.

* * *

When the McClintocks left the Eversons, the sun's last rays were shining through the woods. Parker felt sure that he wasn't going to sleep for a long time that night; he was too happy.

"Here, Parker," his father said, carrying something. "I should never have taken this from you and locked it up."

Seeing the scarlet-colored Bible that his dad was holding, Parker felt the memories of the first time he'd ever walked into church flood back. He remembered Cliff giving him that copy of God's holy word. And he remembered how he'd once tried to hide it himself, pushing it deeply into his closet, not wanting to accept the text within.

"I want you to keep that Bible, Dad," Parker said, locking his gray eyes seriously into Mr. Everson's own. "I have Gwen's now."

Mr. Everson raised his eyebrows in surprise, but then slowly, he nodded. "All right," he replied softly. "Thank you, Son."

"Have a seat, Dad," Parker said, patting the couch cushion at his right. "Don't you think God is incredible? He's always loved us, even when we've scorned Him."

"He truly is longsuffering," Mr. Everson agreed.

"And He's blessed us even when we've suffered," Parker added. "Although we didn't originally want to move, think of what we now have. We've made good friends and found true faith. I still love Wyoming, and I miss our ranch... But I guess we never know what things are before us."

"No, we don't," Mr. Everson agreed. "I often felt isolated in life... especially after Ramona left. But now I see that with the Lord, I'm never alone."

"And just think," Parker said earnestly. "There're Christians all over the world doing the right thing— serving God. Things aren't as dark as they were in Noah's day, when only he and his family were saved in the ark, because everyone else was so wicked."

"That many people being wicked and lost is almost more than I can fathom," Mr. Everson replied. "And just from talking to you, I know I've got a lot of studying to do. Maybe I should start with Noah."

With a laugh, he tilted his head toward the garnet-colored Bible in his hands.

"We can study together," Parker offered happily. He tilted his head to the dark-evergreen-colored Bible. He loved using the very copy that Gwendolyn had so often read from.

"By the way," Parker began, "do you know what my middle name means?"

Shaking his head, his dad replied, "No. Though I really should, since I picked it. I just thought it was a nice sounding name."

"Grace told me that Joshua means 'Jehovah is salvation,'" Parker explained.

"Well, now I like it even more," Mr. Everson replied with a smile. "And there's also a book in the Bible about a man named Joshua, right?"

Parker agreed and then turned to the first chapter of Joshua in his Bible. He was planning to study that book more thoroughly.

Mr. Everson continued, "Hey, so what's my first name mean? Christopher has 'Christ' in it. I'm assuming it has got a spiritual meaning to it."

Jumping up from the couch, Parker then ran to his computer, doing a quick internet search.

"It looks like it means, 'Bearer of Christ,'" Parker answered with a grin. "Today you decided to start living up to your name. Great job, Dad!"

"And it was about time. I don't think my parents were considering the meaning of my name either, son."

Coming back to sit with his dad, Parker then said, "I wonder what Granddad and Grandma are going to think now, once they learn that their son and grandson *both* believe in what they think is fantasy."

"I know they'll still love us. However, they probably won't be exactly... enthused," Mr. Everson stated sadly.

"Yeah... But Luke 12:53 says, *The father shall be divided against the son, and the son against the father; the mother against the daughter, and the daughter against the mother; the mother in law against her daughter in law, and the daughter in law against her mother in law.* I guess we shouldn't be surprised, should we?"

"Did you really just quote that from memory?" Mr. Everson asked, looking astounded.

"Um, yeah, I guess I did," Parker answered taken aback. Without realizing it, he'd already stored that passage away in his heart. "Because I knew you didn't agree with me, I've read it over and over again after my conversion."

"I'm proud of you for standing up for your faith," Mr. Everson said. "Not everyone would do so as willingly as you did. Especially when your grandparents and I tried to talk you out of it. It would have been easy to compromise."

Often, doing the right thing isn't comfortable. There are always sacrifices to make and opportunities to try to please people rather than God. But Christians must press on. They must not let anything, no matter what it may be, take them away from their path of faith. As Matthew 7:13-14 says:

*Enter ye in at the strait gate: for wide is the gate, and broad is the way, that leadeth to destruction, and many there be which go in thereat: Because strait is the gate, and narrow is the way, which leadeth unto life, and few there be that find it.*

It was growing late. Shadows had crawled across the woods and the sky had turned ebony. A half-moon and brilliant stars appeared in the dark blanket. Even so, neither Everson was tired.

"Isn't Sunday going to be nice, Dad?" Parker asked, breaking the stillness that had fallen as they sat and thought.

"It sure will be," Mr. Everson agreed. "You'd better help me though, because I've never so much as walked inside a church building until today."

"Of course, I'll help, Dad!" Parker confirmed, beaming. "It's a wonderful thing, worshiping on Sunday. God really knows everything we need, because not only does He provide for us physically, but He also gives us an abundance of spiritual blessings. Worship honors God while also strengthening us. When I'm at church, I always feel motivated to strive even harder for Christ."

"I'm looking forward to it," Mr. Everson said. "I've spent a lifetime away from the Lord, so I know I've got a lot of learning to do."

"That's right," Parker agreed. "Coming to Christ is a commitment. The word of God changes your life in ways you never thought it could, because, at long last, you have hope. That's a beautiful word, isn't it, Dad? Hope?"

"It sure is, Son," Mr. Everson agreed. "And it's a word I've never fully understood until today."

# A Puzzle Piece with a Purpose

## Chapter 16

The May sun shone brightly on Lake Erie, causing the water to shimmer and scatter light. Swirly clouds stretched across the sky, and a gentle, refreshing breeze flited through the air.

It was a perfect day in late spring. School was out and summer was on the way.

In just a few months, it would be a year since Parker and his dad's move. He was nearly sixteen. Since they'd left the large log cabin nestled in

Wyoming's mountains and entered their small rental in Ohio's suburbs, amid woods and ridges, everything had changed.

What a difference a year could make! When Parker had traveled across America, watching the mountains slowly diminish from sight and entered the terrain of the Midwest, his life had been surrounded in darkness. Now, the light of Christ had burst through the shadows. Parker had never felt such a strong gladness in his heart. Before, he'd had no real reason to love living.

Since it was such a fine day, the McClintocks and Eversons had gotten together to go to the lake. After skipping stones with Jacob for a long time, Parker sat down next to Grace on a large rock. As usual, she'd been content to watch and cheer on their stone skipping competition, rather than joining in herself. But Grace deserved some company, too.

"I'll always remember my first day here," Parker said, gazing out at the long stretch of Lake Erie.

"That was such a fun day," Grace replied softly. "We had the best time showing you around. And I think Jacob and Nana also had the best time skipping stones with you."

"We were all envious of Gwen's throwing arm," Parker replied with a laugh.

"In some ways, it doesn't feel very long ago at all," Grace said, chewing her lip in thought. "But then, at times it feels like an eternity has passed."

"Eternity's a very long time," Parker said, looking at her with a teasing smirk.

"You know what I mean!" Grace laughed, slapping his shoulder, though not painfully.

Becoming serious, Parker then said, "I'm really glad I've met you guys, Grace."

"And we're glad we've met you, likewise," Grace replied, her big blue eyes filled with sincerity. "I'm especially grateful Nana got to know you and even watch you start your journey as a Christian."

"She sure was a good, godly woman," Parker said, sighing. "I'm honored that Gwen gave me her Bible… I love looking at the passages she underlined in it and such."

"It's a treasure, for sure," Grace replied, watching Katie McClintock take photos of the lake. "I think that, like Abel, Nana continues to speak even though she's dead."

"What verse is that?" Parker asked, tilting his head. He hadn't read that passage yet.

"Hebrews 11:4," Grace answered. Then quoting, she said, *"By faith Abel offered unto God a more excellent sacrifice than Cain, by which he obtained witness that he was righteous, God testifying of his gifts: and by it he being dead yet speaketh."*

"I see," Parker responded, meditating on the passage. "So, it means that by Abel's example, his message is still alive?"

"That's right, Parker!" Grace chirped.

"Just like you said, I think Gwen's example—and the message of it—will be imprinted in my mind all the days of my life," Parker explained. "Even when she was gasping for breath, her mind was still on God."

"I have a big middle name to live up to, don't I?" Grace asked.

"You do," Parker agreed. "But I think you're doing a great job at it so far. You never gave up on me, did you? You never stopped trying to teach stubborn old me the truth. For that, I thank you, Grace Elise."

She smiled warmly at him, and then said, "I tried my best to be longsuffering—like God has been to me."

"God's *gracious* to all," Parker said. Then he added with a laugh, "I think it's good your parents named you Grace. Actually, my dad and I were talking about names the day he was converted. It turns out his name means 'Bearer of Christ.' Finally, it fits him!"

Grace tilted her head toward the warm sun, soaking up the pleasures of nature. In the distance, Jacob was striking some silly pose while his mom photographed him by the lake. It was a humorous sight, and light laughter could be heard from Katie.

Turning to Parker, Grace then cheerfully said, "I'm so happy that your dad became a Christian. Keep on keeping on!"

"I will. When I left Wyoming, nothing seemed right," Parker reflected, thinking of those grim days. "Mom's actions had left a deep scar on my family. Dad and I were both struggling to keep it together, and I didn't think I'd ever be happy again. Then, when I met you, it didn't make sense to me why you were so happy all the time, Grace. At first, I thought you'd just had an easy life and looked at the world through rose-colored glasses."

"What do you think now?" Grace asked slyly, smirking.

"I think you're happy because you're good," Parker explained simply. "You live for Christ, and with Christ, no one can truly be sad, because they have an eternal reward."

"If I'm going to be honest, Parker, there are some days when I don't feel happy," Grace began softly. "Sometimes I miss Nana, you know. Or those bullies give me a hard time and make me sad. Or I just feel overwhelmed."

"Everyone has hard days," Parker replied understandingly. "It's how one handles them that sets them apart from the rest."

She nodded, falling silent as she thought of his words.

Continuing, Parker said, "I didn't believe that I'd ever fit in here in Ohio. When you've lived in one place your whole life, you don't always take kindly to change. But also, I didn't think anyone would want to be my friend, because surely they already had enough people in their lives. Forming friendships is a two-way street, as you know."

"I think a lot of people believe they *do* have enough friends," Grace agreed sadly. "It shouldn't be that way, though. Jacob and I wanted to be your friend."

"And look at what that accomplished!" Parker exclaimed enthusiastically. "Thanks to you guys, I learned God's word. Really, I felt like a misplaced puzzle piece back then, when I first moved. Although I was physically in Ohio, I felt like the inner me was stuck in Wyoming, where I thought I belonged."

"And how do you feel now, Parker?"

"I feel like I fit," he replied simply. "I fit in God's heavenly plan."

The two smiled at each other, and then there was another pause of silence. Jacob was still posing ridiculously in the background, almost ruining the moment.

"Actually," Parker said into the quiet, "I just remembered something. There's something I want you to have."

"Oh?" Grace asked, tilting her head.

Pressing a folded piece of notebook paper in her hand, Parker then said, "You've given me notes before. Here's one for you, Grace. Now, what I wrote on the top is a verse I love—and it's one your nana had underlined in her Bible."

Unfolding the paper, Grace then said, "Oh! You've written 1 Peter 5:10."

Parker nodded, and then Grace read the note silently. It read:

*Grace,*

> *"But the God of all grace, who hath called us unto his eternal glory by Christ Jesus, after that ye have suffered a while, make you perfect, stablish, strengthen, settle you." (1 Peter 5:10)*

> *Thank you for never giving up on me. It wasn't until I met you and your family that I really started to think, which is embarrassing to say. Fifteen years is a long time to wait to use your head, wouldn't you say? Since we've become friends, you've done nothing but encourage me every step of the way. For that, I'm always grateful.*

*In Christ,*
*Parker*

"Oh, *Parker*," Grace breathed, her shining blue eyes more vibrant than the azure sky or even Lake Erie. "I'm encouraged by *you*!"

"Even though I was so stubborn at first?" Parker asked with a laugh, surprised.

"Yes," Grace answered firmly. "You didn't brush my words off—even if you wanted to. Instead, you thought about the things I had to say. And watching you overcome your past beliefs to be right with God has strengthened me so much. You've set an incredible example."

"Well, I *needed* to hear what you said," Parker responded. He stared long and hard at Lake Erie, taking in its sheer size, and also thinking about the wonderous Creator.

He recalled when he'd first been at the lake with the McClintocks and how they'd talked about the global flood. Back then, he hadn't believed what they'd discussed. He thought it was nothing more than a fairy tale. But now, he knew how real it truly was.

God had created the world in six days, resting on the seventh. Eventually, man had grown so corrupt that only eight people were righteous. So God flooded the whole earth, only sparing those four men and four women.

This was that same world, hundreds and hundreds of years later. If it hadn't been for Noah, no one would be alive now. Because of the faith of a few, humanity had been spared from utter destruction.

And just as the waters of the flood saved those eight souls from the corruption of man, Christ saves any who believe and obey Him through the waters of baptism. As 1 Peter 3:20-22 says:

*Which sometime were disobedient, when once the longsuffering of God waited in the days of Noah, while the ark was a preparing, wherein few, that is, eight souls were saved by water. The like figure whereunto even baptism doth also now save us (not the putting away of the filth of the flesh, but the answer of a good conscience toward God,) by the resurrection of Jesus Christ: Who is gone into heaven, and is on the right hand of God; angels and authorities and powers being made subject unto him.*

When the world was destroyed through the waters of the flood, that would not be the only time of earth's demolition. One day, God will destroy the world again, but this time permanently and with fire. 2 Peter 3:5-7 reads:

*For this they willingly are ignorant of, that by the word of God the heavens were of old, and the earth standing out of the water and in the water: Whereby the world that then was, being overflowed with water, perished: But the heavens and the earth, which are now, by the same word are kept in store, reserved unto fire against the day of judgment and perdition of ungodly men.*

Judgment Day is coming soon, and no one knows

when. Nobody should delay getting right with God! Eternity is far too long to be separated from Him. Without the Lord, we're lost and condemned. With Him, we're saved and held in His strong hand.

"Hey," Jacob said, coming up to Parker and Grace. "How about we head over to that one ice cream parlor we discovered last month? They sell good mint chocolate chip."

"I'm all for it!" Grace chirped, rising to her feet.

"Me too," Parker replied, also getting up and following them.

Grace smiled at Parker, her blue eyes shining merrily, and she slipped his note into the pocket of her black cargo pants for safe keeping.

Taking a long look at beautiful Lake Erie before he left, Parker sighed contentedly. The seagulls soared across the sapphire sky. A couple of sailboats bobbed like toys across the gentle water.

The teen boy that was overcome with loneliness, feeling lost in a realm of confusion, was gone. Those of the world wouldn't understand what had happened to him, but those in God's family would.

He no longer lived for himself, and he no longer lived for the world. In that lost boy's place was now Parker Everson, a follower of Christ.

At last, Parker was no longer a misplaced puzzle piece. He was held within God's holy hand. In the Lord's picture, Parker was a puzzle piece with a purpose.

Storms would come and darken the blue skies. On earth, Parker's faith would always be tested. But he was equipped with a joy that strengthened him. It is a joy that only those who believe and obey Christ can obtain. If faithful to the Lord until death, he'd be rewarded, as Revelation 2:10 said.

Pulling his eyes away from Lake Erie, Parker sprinted after his friends.

What a joy it is to fit in God's plan.

# A Puzzle Piece with a Purpose

*I cannot fit in this new scene*
*I am a misplaced puzzle piece*
*Your faith I call a fairy tale*
*Yet your joy is hardly frail.*

*Slowly I see the blessed truth*
*But my heart makes petty excuse*
*Though I know it's not a tale*
*I truly fear to cross the vale.*

*The waters wash away my sin*
*Now I start life fresh again*
*Yet Satan wants my soul, he schemes*
*To take my precious faith from me.*

*I fit in this eternal plan!*
*I'm held within God's holy hand*
*Your faith I call reality*
*Devout joy strengthens me.*

Dear Reader,

When I yielded to my holy Savior's will, I was a year younger than Parker Everson. And, in many ways, my upbringing was much like Grace McClintock's. Although the characters in this story are fictional, the message is very real. We all have decisions to make—beliefs we must choose.

God has blessed me with the ability to write *Never a Fairy Tale: A Teen Atheist's Conversion to Christ*. My prayer is that Parker's story will impact you. Perhaps you've loved it; maybe you've hated it. But please never despise the quoted Scriptures within.

If you haven't already, I hope you'll believe in the Lord (John 8:24). I hope you'll repent (Acts 17:30-31). I hope you'll confess Jesus as God's Son (Romans 10:9-10). I hope you'll bury your old self in the waters of baptism and be raised with Christ—just as Jesus was raised for us (Romans 6:4)! What's holding you back? Do you want to be a puzzle piece with a purpose? If so, then obey God's will!

Don't delay. Follow your wonderful Creator and live for Him all the days of your life (2 Timothy 4:7)! He will judge us all (2 Cor. 5:10).

Sincerely,

Danielle Ryce Wallace

## About the Author

DANIELLE RENEE WALLACE is an author born in Washington State. She established an immense love for reading during her elementary school years and a strong passion for writing in middle school. At fourteen, Danielle published her first book while living in Lubbock, Texas. Religion brings meaning to her writing, and she hopes that her life as a follower of Christ will touch others. Danielle was inspired to set *Never a Fairy Tale: A Teen Atheist's Conversion* to Christ in Ohio due to her move there near Lake Erie.

**Other books by Danielle Renee Wallace**


BLOOD FLOWS BLUE SERIES


Escape on the *Honora*

Leaving Midnight Island


SECRETS OF THE ABANDONED BUS SERIES


Lydia Arlington and the Aquarian Mystery

Kodiak Nobleman and the Bull Rider Mystery

Felicia Blackwood and the Remedy Mystery

The Case of 1999

The Charred Warning


For book release updates and more, visit
daniellereneewallace.com